2/0

SHADOWS on the GRASS

Books by *ISAK DINESEN*

Isak Dinesen (*New York*, 1959)

SHADOWS
on the GRASS

by

Karen Blixen

ISAK DINESEN, *pseud.*

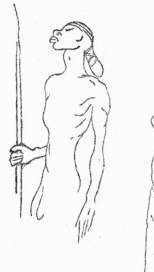

*Masai Moran
and Ndito*

RANDOM HOUSE · *NEW YORK*

Frontispiece portrait of Isak Dinesen by Cecil Beaton; portraits of Abdullahi, Aweru, and an Ndito of the farm by the author.

Poem on pages 102 and 103, by Otto Gelsted, translated by Isak Dinesen.

First published in the United States, 1961

"Barua a Soldani" first appeared in *Esquire* magazine.

MANUFACTURED IN THE UNITED STATES OF AMERICA by Kingsport Press, Inc.

10826

Contents

Illustrations

Farah

As here, after twenty-five years, I again take up episodes of my life in Africa, one figure, straight, candid, and very fine to look at, stands as doorkeeper to all of them: my Somali servant Farah Aden. Were any reader to object that I might choose a character of greater importance, I should answer him that that would not be possible.

Farah came to meet me in Aden in 1913, before the First World War. For almost eighteen years he ran my house, my stables and safaris. I talked to him about my worries as about my successes, and he knew of all that I did or thought. Farah, by the time I had had to give up the farm and was leaving Africa, saw me off in

Mombasa. And as I watched his dark immovable figure on the quay growing smaller and at last disappear, I felt it as if I were losing a part of myself, as if I were having my right hand set off, and from now on would never again ride a horse or shoot with a rifle, nor be able to write otherwise than with my left hand. Neither have I since then ridden or shot.

In order to form and make up a Unity, in particular a creative Unity, the individual components must needs be of different nature, they should even be in a sense contrasts. Two homogeneous units will never be capable of forming a whole, or their whole at its best will remain barren. Man and woman become one, a physically and spiritually creative Unity, by virtue of their dissimilarity. A hook and an eye are a Unity, a fastening; but with two hooks you can do nothing. A right-hand glove with its contrast the left-hand glove makes up a whole, a pair of gloves; but two right-hand gloves you throw away. A number of perfectly similar objects do not make up a whole—a couple of cigarettes may quite well be three or nine. A quartet is a Unity because it is made up of dissimilar instruments. An orchestra is a Unity, and may be perfect as such, but twenty double-basses striking up the same tune are Chaos.

A community of but one sex would be a blind world. When in 1940 I was in Berlin, engaged by three Scandinavian papers to write about Nazi Germany, woman —and the whole world of woman—was so emphatically subdued that I might indeed have been walking about in such a one-sexed community. I felt a relief then, as I watched the young soldiers marching west, to the frontier, for in a fight the adversaries become one, and the two duellists make up a Unity.

The introduction into my life of another race, essentially different from mine, in Africa became to me a mysterious expansion of my world. My own voice and song in life there had a second set to it, and grew fuller and richer in the duet.

Within the literature of the ages one particular Unity, made up of essentially different parts, makes its appearance, disappears and again comes back: that of Master and Servant. We have met the two in rhyme, blank verse and prose, and in the varying costumes of the centuries. Here wanders the Prophet Elisha with his servant Gehazi—between whom one would have supposed the partnership to have come to an end after the affair with Naaman, but whom we meet in a later chapter apparently in the best of understanding. Here walk Terence's Davus and Simo, and Plautus' Calidorus and Pseudolus. Here Don Quixote rides forth, with Sancho Panza on his mule by the croup of Rosinante. Here the Fool follows King Lear across the heath in the storm and the black night, here Leporello waits in the street while inside the palazzo Don Giovanni "reaps his sweet reward." Phileas Fogg struts on to the stage with one single idea in his head and versatile Passepartout at his heels. In our own streets of old Copenhagen Jeronimus and Magdelone promenade arm in arm, while behind their broad and dignified backs Henrik and Pernille make signs to one another.

The servant may be the more fascinating of the two, still it holds true of him as of his master that his play of colours would fade and his timbre abate, were he to stand alone. He needs a master in order to be himself. Leporello, after having witnessed his scapegrace master's lurid end, will still, I believe, from time to time in a circle of friends have produced his list of Don Giovanni's victims and have read out triumphantly: "In Spain are a thousand and three!" The Fool, who is killed by the endless night on the moor, would not have become immortal without the mad old King, to whose lion's roar he joins his doleful, bitter and tender mockery. Henrik and Pernille, if left by Holberg in their own native milieu of Copenhagen valets and ladies' maids, would not have twinkled and sparkled as they do against the background of the sedateness of Jeronimus and Magdelone and the pale romance of Leander and Leonore.

I had in Africa many servants, whom I shall always remember as part of my existence there. There was Ismael, my gun-bearer, a mighty huntsman brought up and trained exclusively in the hunter's world, a great tracker and weather prophet, expressing himself in hunter's terminology and speaking of my "big" and my "young" rifle. It was Ismael who after his return to Somaliland addressed his letter to me "Lioness Blixen" and began it: "Honourable Lioness." There was old Ismael, my cook and faithful companion on safaris, who was a kind of Mohammedan saint. And there was Kamante, a small figure to look at but great, even formidable, in his total isolation. But Farah was my servant by the grace of God.

Farah and I had all the dissimilarities required to make up a Unity: difference of race, sex, religion, milieu and experience. In one thing only were we equal: we had agreed that we were the same age. We were not able to settle the matter exactly, since the Mohammedans reckon with lunar years.

We wander through a long portrait gallery of historical interest: portraits of kings and princes, of great statesmen, poets, and sailors. Amongst all these one face strikes us, an anonymous character, resting in himself, confident of his own nature and dependent on no one. The catalogue that you take up and into which you look tells you: "Portrait of a Gentleman." I shall name my chapter on Farah in an unpretentious way: "Portrait of a Gentleman."

In our day the word "gentleman" is taken less seriously than before, or seems to us to have once taken itself a bit too seriously. But so did Farah take himself seriously.

If the word may be taken to describe or define the person who has got the code of honour of his period and milieu in his own blood, as an instinct—such as the rules of the game will be in the blood of the true cricket or football player, to whom it would not be possible in any situation to throw the ball at the head of his adversary—Farah was the greatest gentleman I have ever met. Only it was, to begin with, difficult to decide what would be the code of honour to a high-born Mohammedan in the house of a European pioneer.

Farah was a Somali, which means that he was no Native of Kenya but an immigrant to the country from Somaliland further north. In my day there were a large number of Somali in Kenya. They were greatly superior to the Native population in intelligence and culture. They were of Arab blood and looked upon themselves as pure-blood Arabs, in some cases even as descendants of the Prophet. On the whole they thought very highly of themselves. They were all fanatical Mohammedans.

The Natives of the land, the Kikuyu, Wakamba, Kawirondo and Masai, have got their own old mysterious and simple cultural traditions, which seem to lose themselves in the darkness of very ancient days. We ourselves have carried European light to the country quite lately, but we have had the means to spread and establish it quickly. In between, an oriental civilization, violent, cruel and very picturesque, gained a foothold in the Highlands through the slave and ivory trade.

The finest ivory in the world comes from East Africa, and the old slave traffic, a long time before the discovery of America, was carried on along these coasts. From here slaves were freighted eastward to Arabia, Persia, India and China, also northward to the Levant; you will see little black Negro pages in old Venetian pictures. From here came the forty black slaves who, together with forty white, carried Aladdin's jewels to the Sultan on their heads. Zanzibar was the great centre of the trade. The Sultan of Zanzibar, I was told when I was there in 1916, was still paid an appanage of £5,000 as compensation for his loss of income from the slave trade. I have seen, at Zanzibar, the market-place and the platform where slaves were put up for sale.

The old commercial intercourse has left its traces in the language of the country. Each tribe of East Africa has got its own language, but all over the Highlands a primitive, ungrammatical lingua franca is spoken: Swahili, the tongue of the coastal tribes. Small children even, herding goats and sheep on the plains, would understand and answer as we asked our way, or questioned them about water or game, in Swahili. I spoke Swahili to my Native servants and labourers on the farm, but as the farm lay in the Kikuyu district, our particular local jargon contained many Kikuyu words and turns of phrase.

The trade also brought the Somali to the country. Most likely Farah's ancestors had been enterprising buyers-up, very likely also hunters and robbers in the Highlands, and possibly pirates on the Red Sea.

The Somali are very handsome people, slim and erect as all East African tribes, with sombre, haughty eyes, straight legs and teeth like wolves. They are vain and have knowledge of fine clothes. When not dressed as Europeans—for many of them would wear discarded suits of their masters' from the first London tailors and would look very well in them—they had on long robes of raw silk, with sleeveless black waistcoats elaborately embroidered in gold. They always wore the turbans of the orthodox Mohammedans in exquisite many-coloured cashmeres; those who had made the pilgrimage to Mecca might wear a green turban.

The dark nations of Africa, strikingly precocious as

young children, seemed to come to a standstill in their mental growth at different ages. The Kikuyu, Kawirondo and Wakamba, the people who worked for me on the farm, in early childhood were far ahead of white children of the same age, but they stopped quite suddenly at a stage corresponding to that of a European child of nine. The Somali had got further and had all the mentality of boys of our own race at the age of thirteen to seventeen. In such young Europeans, too, the code of honour, the deadly devotion to the grand phrase and the grand gesture is the passion urging them on to heroic deeds and heroic self-sacrifice, and also at times sinking them into a dark melancholy and resentment unintelligible to grown-up people. The Somali woman seemed to have stolen a small march upon her male, and from the time when she can first walk until venerable high age presents the picture of the classic *jeune fille* of Europe: coquettish, wily, covetous beyond belief, and sweetly merciful at the core.

I had read the old Nordic Sagas as a child, and now in my intercourse with the Somali I was struck by their likeness to the ancient Icelanders. I was therefore pleased to find Professor Östrup, who is an authority on both nations, making use of a common term to characterize Arabs and Icelanders: he calls them "attitudinizers." The same ravenous ambition to distinguish themselves before all others and at any cost to immortalize themselves through a word or gesture, lies deep in the hearts of the sons of the desert as it did in the hearts of the untamed, salt young seafarers of the Northern Seas.

On the African plains the picture of Ejnar Tambeskälve, the unrivalled young archer, the friend of King Olav Tryggveson, who was with him in the naval battle of Svoldr in the year 1002, was brought back to me. As Ejnar's bowstring burst with a loud boom and the King through the din of the battle cried out: "What burst there so loudly?" he screeched back: "The Kingdom of Norway off thy hand, King Olav!" The wild-eyed warrior boy, standing up straight in the stern of the ship, may have felt with satisfaction that now what was to be achieved had been achieved. And we who today read about him may agree with him, since by now few people will remember who won or lost the battle of Svoldr, or what were the consequences of it, while Ejnar Tambeskälve's *grand mot* has been remembered through a thousand years.

In my dealings with Farah and his tribe I felt that whatever else I might risk from their hand, I did not run the risk of being pitied—no more than I would do in my dealings with a young boy at home.

Personally I have always had a predilection for boys, and have at times reflected that the strong sex reaches its highest point of lovableness at the age of twelve to seventeen—to get it back, in a second flowering, at the age of seventy to ninety. So were the Somali from the first day irresistible to me. With the later European settlers, however, they were not popular.

I myself came out to the Protectorate of British East Africa before the First World War, while the Highlands were still in very truth the happy hunting-grounds, and while the white pioneers lived in guileless harmony with the children of the land. Most of the immigrants had come to Africa, and had stayed on there, because they liked their African existence better than their existence at home, would rather ride a horse than go in a car and rather make up their own campfire than turn on the central heating. Like me they wished to lay their bones in African soil. They were almost all themselves country-bred and open-air people; many of them were younger sons of old English families, schooled early in life by elderly, dignified keepers and stablemen and were accustomed to proud servants. Themselves untamed, with fresh hearts, they were capable of forming a Hawkeye-Chingachgook fellowship with a dark, untamed nomad or hunter; they accepted and trusted the Somali, as the Somali accepted and trusted them.

During the war, and the first years after it, no new settlers landed. But in the following years an energetic advertising of the Colony of Kenya as a country of unique economic possibilities was started in England, and "Closer Settlement" was made the catchword. It brought out a new class of settlers, people who had grown up and lived in one town or one community in England, and who were strangely provincial compared to the African Natives, who were at any time prepared for anything. Plots of land were also given out as rewards to British non-commissioned officers, most of whom were city people, who in the loneliness of the great landscapes felt that they had been promised more than they were given.

To me it was a sad programme. From the point of view of emigration, I reflected, Kenya, with an altitude and a climate in which white people could not take on manual labour, and with a vast Native population, would never be an area of great moment. When I first came to the country there were about five thousand white people there; she might, I thought, possibly take in ten times as many. But then, I was told, Australia and New Zealand and Canada could at the same time take in up to fifty or a hundred millions. And from the point of view of the country itself, the "true home of my heart," a closer white settlement was a dubious benefit, and it was the quality, not the quantity of white settlers which we should have at heart. I laugh, and I suppose I ought to blush, when I call to mind that at this time I wrote to a very superior political personage in England and developed my views to him. I am indeed touched when I remember that he did really send an answer to my letter, in a courteous, if non-committal note.

To these later arrivals to the country the Somali, her

earliest immigrants, seemed haughty and unmanage-
able and were, I believe, on the whole as intolerable as
to me and my friends they were indispensable. So it
came that our particular clan of early settlers—arro-
gantly looking upon ourselves as Mayflower people—
might be characterized as those Europeans who kept
Somali servants and to whom a house without a Somali
would be like a house without a lamp. Here were Lord
Delamere and Hassan, Berkeley Cole and Jama, Denys
Finch-Hatton and Bilea, and I myself and Farah. We
were the people who, wherever we went, were followed,
at a distance of five feet, by those noble, vigilant and
mysterious shadows.

Berkeley Cole and I, in a private jargon of ours, distinguished between respectability and decency, and
divided up our acquaintances, human and animal, in
accordance with the doctrine. We put down domestic
animals as respectable and wild animals as decent,
and held that, while the existence and prestige of the
first were decided by their relation to the community,
the others stood in direct contact with God. Pigs and
poultry, we agreed, were worthy of our respect, inasmuch as they loyally returned what was invested in

them, and in their most intimate private life behaved as was expected of them. We watched them in their sties and yards, perseveringly working at the return of investments made, pleasantly feeding, grunting and quacking. And leaving them there, to their own homely, cosy atmosphere, we turned our eyes to the unrespectable, destructive wild boar on his lonely wanderings, or to those unrespectable, shameless corn-thieves, the wild geese and duck, in their purposeful line of flight across the sky, and we felt their course to have been drawn up by the finger of God.

We registered ourselves with the wild animals, sadly admitting the inadequacy of our return to the community—and to our mortgages—but realizing that we could not possibly, not even in order to obtain the highest approval of our surroundings, give up that direct contact with God which we shared with the hippo and the flamingo. Nine thousand feet up we felt safe, and we laughed at the ambition of the new arrivals, of the Missions, the business people and the Government itself, to make the continent of Africa respectable. A time came when we began to feel uneasy about the matter. The Protestant Missions gave much time, energy and money to make the Natives put on trousers—in which they looked like giraffes in harness. The French Fathers were in better understanding with the children of the land, but they did not have—as they ought to have had—Saint Francis of Assisi at their Mission station; they were themselves but frail souls, and at home had been loaded with a heavy, mixed cultural cargo, which they dared not throw off. The businessmen, under the motto of "Teach the Native to Want," encouraged the African to evaluate himself by his possessions and to keep up respectably with his neighbours. The Government, turning the great wild plains into game Reserves, seemed to succeed in making the lions themselves take on the look of kindly patresfamilias— times might come when our old feline friends would have their regular meals served them from Game Department canteens. It was doubtful whether sans them the graminivora would preserve their innocence of the period before the Fall, whether then the kongoni would still keep their lonely watcher silhouetted on top of a hill, the eland their silky skin swaying in the dewlap as they trotted along, and their moist eyes, the impala their flying leap. Must there then, even in Africa, be no live creature standing in direct contact with God?

Ay, but there will be, I consoled myself, as long as I have got Farah with me. For Farah, although gravely posing as a highly respectable major-domo, Malvolio himself, was a wild animal, and nothing in the world would ever stand between him and God. Unfailingly loyal, he was still at heart a wild animal, a cheetah noiselessly following me about at a distance of five feet, or a falcon holding on to my finger with strong talons and turning his head right and left. The qualities with which he served me were cheetah or falcon qualities.

When Farah first took service in my house, or first took my house into possession—for from that day he spoke of "our house," "our horses," "our guests"—it was no common contract which was set up, but a covenant established between him and me *ad majorem domus gloriam,* to the ever greater glory of the house. My well-being was not his concern, and was hardly of real importance to him, but for my good name and prestige he did, I believe, hold himself responsible before God.

Farah was a highly picturesque figure in my house as he stepped forth on its threshold. In his relations with my Native servants he was unwaveringly fair and impartial, and he had a deeper knowledge of them and their course of thought than I could well account for, for I hardly ever saw him converse with them. Farah spoke English correctly, and French as well, for he had in his young days been cabin-boy on a French man-of-war, but he had a few expressions of his own which I ought to have set him right about, but which instead in our talks together I took to using myself. He said "exactly" for "except": "All the cows have come home exactly the grey cow," and I still at times find myself making use of the word in the same way.

Farah had the typical Somali voice, recognizable among all voices of the world, low, guttural, with a two-fold ring to it, for it was friendly but lent itself excellently well to a particular contempt or scorn. At times Farah like most Somali annoyed me by having so little *Gemütlichkeit* in his mental make-up. I accounted for it by the tribes' abstinence from wine or spirits through a thousand years, and reflected that the sight of an old uncle dead drunk would have been a wholesome remedy against the desert dryness of the Somali mind.

He once told me that he did not like the Jews because they "ate antruss," and for a while I wondered which would be the food that shocked him in the Jews, since the pork forbidden to Mohammedans is forbidden to the children of Israel as well. In the end, however, I gathered from him that what roused his indignation was the Jewish practice of charging interest on money lent, a proceeding forbidden to and despised by the Mohammedans. He said of an ambitious English friend of the house: "He never get Sir," meaning that he would never obtain the honour of being knighted. At the time when the locusts came upon us the Natives roasted and ate them; I had a mind to try them myself, but still somehow doubtful asked Farah what they tasted like. "I know not, Memsahib," he answered, "I eat not such small birds." He had a partiality for the demonstrative adjective: "This Arab horse dealer offers you this horse at this price," and rarely spoke about his fellow-men but in the same way: "this Kamante," "this Prince of Wales."

Thomas Mann in his book *Joseph in Egypt* tells us that the ancient Egyptians had the same usage, and that Joseph taught himself to speak according to their taste: "As we came to this fortress this good old man said to this officer." It may be a particular African inclination.

Farah strictly saw to it that our Native servants groomed the horses and polished the silver of the house till they shone. He drove my old Ford car as if it had been a Rothschild's Rolls-Royce. And he expected from me a corresponding loyalty to the paragraphs of our covenant. As a consequence of this attitude he was a highly expensive functionary in the house, not only because his salary was disproportionately larger than that of my other servants, but because he did without mercy demand my house to be run in grand style.

Farah was my cashier, he had charge of all money I took home from the bank and of my keys. He never drew up any accounts for me and would hardly have been able to do so, nor would it ever have occurred to me to demand it from him. I never doubted but that he did to the best of his ability spend my money in the interest of my house. Only there always remained to me a strong exciting element of suspense as to his views of the interests of the house.

I once asked him: "Farah, can you give me five rupees?" And he asked me in return: "What do you want them for, Memsahib?" "I want to buy a new pair of slacks," I said. Farah shook his head. "We cannot afford that this month, Memsahib," he said. He told me: "I pray to God that your old riding-boots may last till your new ones arrive out from London." Farah had good knowledge of riding-boots and felt it to be below my dignity to walk about in boots made by the Indians of Nairobi.

To make up for it he was liberal in other matters. He decreed: "We must have champagne for dinner tonight, Memsahib." My English friends, who in between their long safaris stayed in my house, kept it in wine at a very high standard, but it happened when they were away for a long time that I ran short of wine. "We have got so little champagne left, Farah," I said. "We must have champagne," Farah said again. "Have you forgotten, Memsahib, that there is a Memsahib coming for dinner?" My guests as a rule were men.

Farah

When Prince Wilhelm of Sweden was coming for tea to the farm, in his honour I wanted to make a kind of Swedish cake called *Klejner,* for which you need a little bit, what the cookery-books call a pinch, of cardamom. As Farah was going to Nairobi I added the cardamom to his shopping list. "I do not know," I said, "whether the white grocers will have it. But if you cannot get it with them you must go to the Indians." The great Indian tradesmen, Suleiman Virjee and Allidina Visram, were personal friends of Farah's and owned more than half of the native trade-quarter, which was called the Bazaar.

Farah came back late in the evening and reported: "This precious spice, Memsahib, which other Europeans do not know, but which we must have, was very difficult to get. First I went to these white grocers, but they had not got it. Then I went to Suleiman Virjee, and he had it. And then I bought for five hundred rupees." A rupee was two shillings. "You are crazy, Farah," I said. "I meant you to buy for ten cents." "You did not tell me so," said Farah. "No, I did not tell you so," I said. "I thought you had human intelligence. But in any case I have no use for five hundred rupees' worth of cardamom, and you will have to give it back to Suleiman Virjee where you got it." I at once realized that it would be impossible to make Farah carry out my order. It was not the inconvenience that he feared, for no kind of inconvenience means anything to a Somali. But he would not allow Suleiman Virjee to believe that a house like ours could do with less then five hundred rupees' worth of cardamom.

He thought the matter over and said: "No. No, that would not be good, Memsahib. But I will tell you what we will do. I shall take over this lot." So we left it at that, and the Somali are such furious tradespeople that Farah at once got the hitherto unknown article introduced on the farm, so that soon every self-esteeming Kikuyu went about chewing cardamom and dashingly spitting out the capsules. I tried it myself and it was not bad. I feel that Farah will have made a handsome profit on the transaction.

Farah's knowledge of Native mentality came in useful to me.

Once, at the end of a month, when I had been paying out their wages to my people on the farm, in going through my accounts I found that a hundred-rupee note was missing and must have been stolen. I passed on the sad news to Farah, and he at once very calmly declared that he would get me my money back. "But how?" I asked him. "There have been more than a thousand people up here, and we have no idea at all as to who may be the thief." "Nay, but I will get you your money back," said Farah.

He walked away, and towards evening returned carrying with him a human skull. This may sound highly dramatic, but was in itself nothing out of the normal. For centuries the Natives had not buried their dead but had laid them out on the plain where jackals and vultures would take care of them. One might at any time, riding or walking there, in the long grass knock against an amber-coloured thigh-bone or a honey-brown skull.

Farah rammed down a pole outside my door and nailed the skull to the top of it. I stood by and watched him without enthusiasm. "What is the good of that, Farah?" I asked him. "The thief will already be far away. And must I now have that skull of yours set up just outside my door?" Farah did not answer, he took a step back to survey his work and laughed. But next morning, by the foot of the pole a stone was lying, and underneath it a hundred-rupee note. By what dark, crooked paths it had got there I was not told, and now shall never know.

Farah, as already told, was a strict Mohammedan, burning in the spirit.

In speaking about Mohammedans and Mohammedanism, I am well aware that I got to know in Africa only a primitive, unsophisticated Mohammedanism. Of Mohammedan philosophy or theology I know nothing; from my own experience I can but tell how Islam manifests itself in the course of thought and conduct of the unlearned Orthodox. All the same I feel that you cannot live for a long time among Mohammedans without your own view of life being in some way influenced by theirs.

I have been told that the word "Islam" in itself means submission: the Creed may be defined as the religion which ordains acceptance. And the Prophet does not accept with reluctance or with regret but with rapture. There is in his preaching, as I know it from his unlearned disciples, a tremendous erotic element.

"Sweet scents, incense and perfumes are dear to my

heart," says the Prophet. "But the glory of women is dearer. The glory of women is dear to my heart. But the glory of prayer is dearer."

In contrast to many modern Christian ideologies, Islam does not occupy itself with justifying the ways of God to man; its Yes is universal and unconditional. For the lover does not measure the worth of his mistress by a moral or social rod. But the mistress, by absorbing into her own being the dark and dangerous phenomena of life, mysteriously transluminates and sanctifies them, and imbues them with sweetness. An old Danish love poem has it: "There is witchcraft on your lips, an abyss within your gaze." What the wooer desires is freedom to adore, what he craves and thirsts for is the assurance of being loved back. Kadidja's caravaneer, with his eyes on the new moon, in the words of a later author, even though in a somewhat altered sense, is "God's own mad lover, dying on a kiss."

I sometimes wondered whether the tribes of the desert had become what they were by having been in the hand of the Prophet for twelve hundred years, or whether his Creed has taken such deep roots in them because from the very beginning they were of one blood with him. I imagined that just as the erotic aloofness of the founder of Christianity has left his disciples in a kind of void, or of chronic uneasiness and remorse, within this province of life, so has the formidable, indomitable potency of the Prophet pervaded his followers and made mighty latent forces in them fetch headway. Eroticism runs through the entire existence of the great wanderers. Horses and camels are desirable and exquisite possessions in a man's life, and well worth that he should risk it for their sake. But they cannot compete or compare with women. To the hearts of the ascetic, hardened, ruthless tribes it is the number and the quality of the wives which decides a man's success and happiness in life, and his own worth.

When, on the farm, I was called upon to give judgment in matters between my Mohammedan people, I looked up rules and regulations in the manual of Mohammedan law, *Minhaj et Talibin*. It is a thick and heavy, highly imposing book to have carried about with you, a surprising work as well to a North European mind in its taboos and recommendations, enlightening as to the Mohammedan view of life, infinitely detailed in its regulations on legal purity, prayer, fasting and

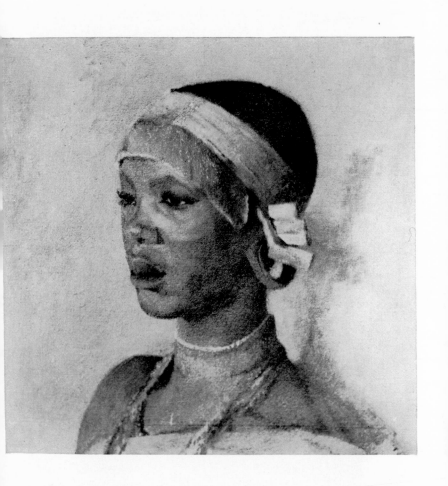

Kikuyu Ndito from the Ngong farm

distribution of alms and particularly upon woman and her position in the community of the Orthodox. "The law," the classic states, "forbids a man to clothe himself in silk. But a woman may wear clothes of silk and should do so whenever this be in all decency possible to her." The Somali whom I knew did, however, wear silk, but Farah explained to me that they would do so only when outside their own country and in the service of other people—and surely my old valued friend Ali bin Salim of Mombasa, or the old Indian high priest who came to see me on the farm, wore but the finest and most delicate wools. The book also lays down as law that a husband shall supply his wife not only with the necessary nourishment, lodgings and clothes, but that he shall also give her such and such luxuries, within his means, which are truly worthy of her and will make her truly value her husband. "In the case, however," it adds, "of a woman of remarkable beauty, jurists may find themselves not entirely in accordance and will have to weigh the matter between them." The very grave and somewhat pedantic book thus registers woman's beauty as an indisputable, juridical asset in existence.

They rush forth, these warriors of the great fantasias, to meet the will of God—his adorable will—as the Jews rush forth to meet the Sabbath: "Get thee up, brethren, to welcome the bride!" Or David, King of Israel, in his Psalm 119: "O how love I thy law!" They are a communion of yes-sayers, they are in love with danger, with death and with God.

As Job's laments are not silenced by expositions of the justice and mercy of God, but it is before the revelation of God's greatness that the complainer surrenders and consents, the Prophet surrenders and consents: "God is great." In the same way did Farah consent, when after three weeks' hard tracking we came up close to a herd of elephants and I shot and missed, and the elephants marched away so that we never saw them again. In the same way did he consent when in a year of drought, news was brought him from Somaliland that half his camels had perished, and when I told him of Denys Finch-Hatton's death: "God is great."

It is a general notion among Christians that Mohammedanism is more intolerant than Christianity, but such is not my own experience. There were three great prophets—*Nebbes*—Farah told me, Mohammed, Jesus and Moses. He would not recognize Christ as the Son of God, for God could have no son in the flesh, but he would agree that he had no human father. He named him Isa ben Mariammo. About Mariammo he spoke much, praising her beauty and virginity—she had, he said, been walking in her mother's garden when an angel had brushed her shoulder with his wing; through this she had conceived. He smacked his own small son Saufe because he repeated some words of abuse about the Virgin which naughty Kikuyu totos from the Scotch Mission had taught him.

When in the thirties I was staying in the south of England with Denys' brother, the Earl of Winchilsea, the painter John Philpot came down to paint the portrait of my hostess, who was very lovely. He had travelled much in North Africa, and on an afternoon when we were walking together in the park he recounted to me an experience of his from there.

In the First World War, he said, he had had a shell-shock or a nervous breakdown; he would never feel sure that he was doing what he ought to do.

"When I was painting a picture," he explained, "I

felt that I ought to make up my bank account. When I was making up my bank account, I felt that I ought to go for a walk. And when, in a long walk, I had got five miles away from home, I realized that I ought to be, at this very moment, in front of my easel. I was constantly in flight, an exile everywhere.

"It happened by then that I and my African servant in our travels in Morocco came to a small town or village. I cannot really describe the place to you, it looked like any other North African village. It stood in a flat plain, and in itself it was nothing but a number of mud-built huts with an old, broad mud-built wall round it. The only particular thing that I remember about it is its great multitude of storks, a stork's nest on almost every house. But at the moment when I had come through the gate in the wall I felt that this was a place of refuge. There came upon me a strange, blissful calm, a happiness like what you feel when a high fever leaves you. 'Here,' I thought, 'one can remain.'

"And as now I had stayed in the village for a fort-night, all the time in that same sweet peace of soul and giving no thought to the past or the future, on a day when I was once more painting a picture, an old man, a priest, came up and spoke to me. 'I hear from your servant,' he said, 'that you have finished your wanderings and will stay with us, since here you have found rest.' I answered him that it was as he said, but that I could not explain to myself why it should be so.

" 'Master,' said the old man, 'I shall explain it to you. There is something special about our village, things have happened here that have happened nowhere else. It came about, not when I was a boy myself but when my father was a boy of twelve, and he has related it to me as it happened. Turn your eyes to the gate in the wall behind us. Above it you will see a ledge, where two men can sit, for in old days watchmen were here looking out for foes that might approach across the plain. To this very ledge above the gate came the Prophet himself and your Prophet Jesus Christ. They met here to talk together of man's lot on earth and of the means by which the people of the earth might be helped. Those standing down below could not hear what they said to one another. But they could see the Prophet, as he explained his thoughts, striking his hand against his knee, and thereupon Jesus Christ lifting his hand and answering him. They sat there, deep in talk, till night fell and the people could no longer see them. And it is from that time, Master, that our village has got peace of heart to give away.'

"I wonder," said Mr. Philpot, "whether a clergyman of the Church of England would have told that tale."

Like all Mohammedans Farah was without fear. Europeans call the Islamitic view of life fatalism. I myself do not think that the Prophet's followers see the happenings of life as predestined and therefore inescapable. They are fearless because confident that what happens is the best thing.

Farah, in one of my first years in Africa, stood beside me when a wounded lion charged—"charged home" as hunters say, meaning that now only death will stop him. Farah had no rifle with him, and at that time, I believe, but slight faith in my marksmanship. But he did not move, I do not think that he winced. Good luck had it that in my second shot I hit the lion so that he rolled over like a hare, then Farah very quietly walked up to him and inspected him.

At a later time, though, to my surprise I heard Farah speak in deep admiration of my skill with a rifle. During one of our long safaris, when in the morning after a night's shooting I was still in bed in my tent, a young Englishman who had his camp some miles south of ours, and who had heard about us from the Natives, came over to enquire about water and game and to have company. He and Farah were talking together outside the tent, and I could follow their conversation through the canvas. "What kind of Bwana are you out with?" the Englishman asked. "Is he a good shot, and are you getting anything?" "I am with no Bwana," Farah answered, "but with a Memsahib from a distant country. And she never misses a thing."

On this occasion Farah seemed to enjoy talking about me. Generally the Somali will not discuss women and you cannot make them tell you of their wives and daughters. Only in regard to their mothers do they make an exception, and the Koran, Farah said, orders that each time you name your father with reverence you should name your mother with reverence twenty-five times. In this point as in others the Somali are like the old Icelanders. Tormod Kolbrunnaskjald was exiled from Iceland because he had sung the girl he loved, naming her "Kolbrunna."

It is a strange thing that I should have this taboo in

me still. At times, when people speak or write about me, I feel that I am breaking my covenant with Farah.

When the Prince of Wales, the present Duke of Windsor, in 1928 came on his first visit to Kenya, I had been invited by my friend Joanie Grigg, the Governor's wife, to stay for a week at Government House. I felt that this was an opportunity of bringing the cause of the Natives, in the matter of their taxation, before the Prince, and was happy about this chance of getting the ear of the future King of England. "Only," I said to myself, "it will have to be done in a pleasant manner. For if it does not amuse him he will do nothing about it."

As I sat beside the Prince at dinner I cautiously tried to turn his interest the way I wanted, and he did indeed on the next day come out to the farm to have tea with me. He walked with me into the huts of the squatters and made enquiries as to what they possessed in the way of cattle and goats, what they might earn by working on the farm and what they paid in taxes, writing down the figures. It was to me later on, when I was back in Denmark, a heart-breaking thing that my Prince of Wales should be King of England for only six months.

In the course of another evening I had been describing to the Prince the big Ngomas on the farm, and as he said good-night to me he added: "I should like to dine with you on Friday and to see such an Ngoma." This was Tuesday night, and for the next two days the Prince would be up at Nanyuky for the races.

When I came up to my rooms in Government House I found Farah there waiting for orders for the morrow, for you always bring your own servant with you when staying in the houses of your friends. I said to him: "Something terrible has happened to us, Farah. The Prince is coming out on Friday to dine and to see our people dance. And you know that they will not dance at this time of the year." For these Ngomas were ritual dances connected with the harvest, and all settlers knew well enough that in this matter the Natives would rather die than break with a sacred law of a thousand years.

Farah was as deeply shaken by the news as I myself. For a few minutes he was struck dumb and turned into stone. In the end he spoke. "If it be indeed so, Memsahib," he said, "to my mind there is only one thing for us to do. I shall take the car and go round to the big

Chiefs. I shall speak to them and tell them that now they must come to help you. I shall remind them that three months ago you helped them." I had had the luck to be able to assist the Natives in a matter between them and the Government concerning salt-rocks to which they had formerly brought their cattle to lick salt. "But then," Farah added with some misgiving, "I can do nothing about this dinner. You will have to look after that, with Kamante, Memsahib." There was some distance and hardly any roads between the manyattas of the great Chiefs, and the old men would seize this opportunity to talk. I answered: "Nay, give no thought to that. I and Kamante will be able to look after it. For I think that you are right and that this is the best thing we can do."

I returned to the farm to make preparations for Friday with a somewhat heavy heart, and Farah drove out from it, an ambassador on a tricky mission. When on the morning of Friday he was not back, the entire household, preparing the lobster up from Mombasa, the spurfowl brought in by Masai Morani, and Kamante's Cumberland sauce for the ham, was dead silent. It would be a dark, eternal shame to our house and to all of us, were the prince to come out to see an Ngoma, and we to have no Ngoma to show him.

But already at eight or nine o'clock our own young men and girls of the farm began to hang round the house, in the mysterious way of the Natives aware that great things were about to happen. During the next few hours dance-loving young people from farms further away followed, coming up the long avenue in small groups. Kamante, for once taking an optimistic view of a situation, remarked to me that this was like the time when the locusts came: one by one, then a number together, then in the end more than we would be able to count. At eleven o'clock we heard the car coming up the drive asthmatically. She was all plastered in mud and dust, and Farah himself as he stepped out of her seemed to have faded, in the way of dark people when thoroughly exhausted. I felt that all through these two nights he must have sat up in unceasing palaver with the old Chiefs. Yet at the very first glance we all knew him to have come back victorious.

"Memsahib," he said in a voice almost as hoarse as

that of the car, "they are coming. They are coming all of them, and they are bringing with them their young men and their virgins."

They did indeed follow close on the track of the car, swarming, as Kamante had predicted it, locust-like, a stream of supple, fiery young people of both sexes, set on dancing, should it cost them their life. The small groups of an old Chief and his aged counsellors, in rich, heavy monkey-skin cloaks, advanced in state, isolated from the common crowd by ten feet of empty space before and after them.

That night there were between two and three thousand dancers at the dancing-place by my house. The moon was full, and there was no breath of wind, the circle of small fires blazed and glowed a long way into the woods and sent up thin columns of smoke towards the sky. It was a fine Ngoma, I have seen no finer anywhere.

The Prince made the tour of the forest ball-room, stopping to speak to the old Chiefs one after the other. He spoke to them in Swahili, and they, hanging on to their sticks, gave him their answers keenly from smiling, toothless mouths, after which, for obvious reasons, the conversation ceased. He made an impression on the Ancients; afterwards they liked to speak about him. Africans laugh for reasons different from those of Europeans, most often from sheer spite but often also from mere content—for a long time they laughed when they spoke of the Prince, as if we had been discussing a very precious baby. I believe that the Prince himself was pleased with his Ngoma.

A fortnight later I again sent for the Kikuyu Chiefs. I had, I said to them, on the day of the Ngoma found myself in a difficult position, I had asked them to help me and they had helped me, now I wanted to thank them. I handed over a present to each of them, but by now I do not remember whether of a particularly fine rug or a goat.

A very old man, after they had had a few minutes to let my message sink into them, came up and spoke to me. "Now you have told us, Msabu," he said, "that on the day of the great Ngoma you found yourself in difficult position, and you asked us to help you and we helped you. Now you wanted to thank us, so you have given each of us a present. May we now say something to you?" This is a common address with Natives; you

ISAK DINESEN

cannot well refuse the request, but after it you will have
to be prepared for anything. I told the old man that he
was free to say to me what he liked. "Msabu," he said
with much weight and satisfaction. "I shall, then, like
to tell you something of which among ourselves we have
talked much, and about which we are happy. We think
that on the night when the Toto a Soldani came here
to see our young men and virgins dance, among the
Msabus present you had on the nicest frock. It pleased
our hearts, Msabu, it still pleases our hearts when we
think about it. For we all think that here, every day on
the farm, you are terribly badly dressed."

I did not contradict him. Generally on the farm I
wore old khaki slacks stained with oil, mud and fouling.
I felt that my people had dreaded, that upon a historical
occasion on the farm and at a moment when I had
called upon them to do their utmost, to see me let them
down.

For the sake of my female readers I shall here insert
that at the time of the Prince's visit I had not been to
Europe for four years and could have no real idea as to
what fashions there were like. So I asked the house in
Paris, which had got my measures and was to make my

44

frock, to follow their own notions about what would be truly chic. *"Nous sommes convaincus, Madam,"* they wrote back, *"que vous serez la plus belle."* They had had the good sense to make me, in the heyday of the chemise frock—which was nothing but two vertical lines starting below the armpits and cut off above the knee—a so-called *robe de style* not likely to go out of fashion, with a hooped skirt of great fullness, in silver brocade. I think that it pleased the hearts of my people to see me, among the lank women of the dinner party, suddenly swell out to an unexpected voluminousness.

As now the old Chiefs and I in our talk together had got on to that very pleasant theme of my frock, I wanted to hear more of what they thought about it. But at this moment Farah stepped on to the stage, followed by Kamante carrying a wooden bowl that contained tombacco—snuff—for my guests. He looked approving but stern. He was not insensitive to popularity, but he was resolved on keeping the Kikuyu in their place, and me in mine.

"Wait a little, Farah," I said. "I am talking with the old people, they are talking with me."

"No, Memsahib," said Farah. "No. Now these Kikuyus have said enough about this frock. Now it is time that they have this tombacco."

Then came the hard times on the farm, and my certainty that I could not keep it. And then began my ever-repeated travels to Nairobi with such sorry aims as keeping my creditors quiet, obtaining a better price for the farm and, at the very end, after I had in reality lost the farm and become, so to say, a tenant in my own house, securing for my squatters the piece of land in the Reserve where according to their wish they could remain together. It took a long time before I could make the Government consent to my scheme. On these expeditions Farah was always with me.

And now it happened that he unlocked and opened chests of which till then I had not known, and displayed a truly royal splendour. He brought out silk robes, gold-embroidered waistcoats, and turbans in glowing and burning reds and blues, or all white—which is a rare thing to see and must be the real gala head-dress of the Somali—heavy gold rings and knives in silver- and ivory-mounted sheaths, with a riding whip of giraffe hide inlaid with gold, and in these things he looked like the Caliph Harun-al-Rashid's own bodyguard. He followed me, very erect, at a distance of five feet, where I walked, in my old slacks and patched shoes, up and down Nairobi streets. There he and I became a true Unity, as picturesque, I believe, as that of Don Quixote and Sancho Panza. There he lifted up me and himself to a classic plane, such as that of which the Norwegian poet Wergeland speaks:

Death follows the happy man like a stern master,
The unfortunate like a servant,
Who is ever ready to receive his master's cloak and
  mask.

When I had sold all the contents of my house, my panelled rooms became sounding-boards. If I sat down on one of the packing-cases containing things to be sent off, which were now my only furniture, voices and tunes of old rang through the nobly bare room intensified, clear. When during these months a visitor came to the farm, Farah stood forth, holding open the door to the empty rooms as if he had been doorkeeper to an imperial palace.

No friend, brother or lover, no nabob suddenly presenting me with the amount of money needed to keep the farm, could have done for me what my servant Farah then did. Even if I had got nothing else for which to be grateful to him—but that I have got, and more than I can set down here—I should still for the sake of these months, now, thirty years after, and as long as I live, be in debt to him.

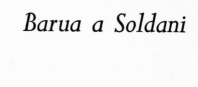

Barua a Soldani

Readers of my book *Out of Africa* may remember how, on a New Year's morning, before sunrise—while the stars, on the point of withdrawing and vanishing into the dome of the sky, were still hanging on it like big luminous drops, and the air still had in it the strange limpidity and depth, like well water, of African dawn— together with Denys Finch-Hatton and his Kikuyu chauffeur, Kanuthia, I was driving along a very bad road in the Masai Reserve, and there shot a lion upon a dead giraffe.

Later on Denys and I were accused of having shot the giraffe, a thing not allowed by the game laws. The Game Department in your shooting licence gave you the right to hunt, shoot or capture so and so many head of such and such game—I sometimes wondered by what right the Game Department dealt out such rights—and the giraffe was not included. Lions, however, you might shoot at any time, within the distance of thirty miles to a farm. But Kanuthia could bear us up in our statement that the giraffe had been dead a day or two before we came upon it.

I do not know whether the lion had actually killed the giraffe. Lions kill by breaking the necks of their victims, and in view of the height of a giraffe's shoulders and neck the thing seems unlikely. On the other hand the strength and energy of a lion are indeed incredible things, and hunters have solemnly assured me that they have seen giraffes being killed by lions.

The squatters on my farm during the past three months had been up to the house begging me to shoot a lion *"mbaya sana"*—very bad—which was following and worrying their herds. The lion that I met this morning and which, even on our close approach, remained on the back of his prey, absorbed in his meal and one with it, and only slightly stirring in the dim air, might well be the very same killer, the cause of so much woe over precious cows and bullocks. We were about twenty miles from the border of the farm, but a distance of twenty miles means nothing to a lion. If it were he, ought I not to shoot him when he himself gave me the chance? Denys, as Kanuthia slowed down the car, whispered to me: "You shoot this time." I had not got my own rifle with me, so he handed me his. I was never keen to shoot with his rifle, it was too heavy and in particular too long for me. But my old friend, Uncle Charles Bulpett, had told me: "The person who can take delight in a sweet tune without wanting to learn it, in a beautiful woman without wanting to possess her, or in a magnificent head of game without wanting to shoot it, has not got a human heart." So that the shot, here before daybreak, was in reality a declaration of love—and ought not then the weapon to be of the very first quality?

Or it may be said that hunting is ever a love-affair. The hunter is in love with the game, real hunters are true animal lovers. But during the hours of the hunt itself he is more than that, he is infatuated with the head of game which he follows and means to make his own; nothing much besides it exists to him in the world.

Only, in general, the infatuation will be somewhat one-sided. The gazelles and antelopes and the zebra, which on safari you shoot to get meat for your porters, are timid and will make themselves scarce and in their own strange way disappear before your eyes; the hunter must take wind and terrain into account and sneak close to them slowly and silently without their realizing the danger. It is a fine and fascinating art, in the spirit of that masterpiece of my countryman Sören Kierkegaard, *The Seducer's Diary*, and it may, in the same way, provide the hunter with moments of great drama and with opportunity for skill and cunning, and for self-gratulations. Yet to me this pursuit was never the real thing. And even the big game, in the hunting of which there is danger, the buffalo or the rhino, very rarely attack without being attacked, or believing that they are being attacked.

Elephant-hunting is a sport of its own. For the elephant, which through centuries has been the one head of game hunted for profit, in the course of time has adopted man into his scheme of things, with deep distrust. Our nearness to him is a challenge which he will never disregard; he comes towards us, straightly and

quickly, on his own, a towering, overwhelming struc-
ture, massive as cast iron and lithe as running water.
"What time he lifteth up himself on high, the mighty
are afraid." Out go his ears like a dragon's wings, giving
him a grotesque likeness to the small lap-dog called a
papillon; his formidable trunk, crumpled up accordion-
like, rises above us like a lifted scourge. There is passion
in our meeting, positiveness on both sides; but on his
side there is no pleasure in the adventure, he is driven
on by just wrath, and is settling an ancient family feud.

In very old days the elephant, upon the roof of the
earth, led an existence deeply satisfying to himself and
fit to be set up as an example to the rest of creation:
that of a being mighty and powerful beyond anyone's
attack, attacking no one. The grandiose and idyllic
modus vivendi lasted till an old Chinese painter had his
eyes opened to the sublimity of ivory as a background
to his paintings, or a young dancer of Zanzibar hers to
the beauty of an ivory anklet. Then they began to appear to all sides of him, small alarming figures in the
landscape drawing closer: the Wanderobo with his
poisoned arrows, the Arab ivory-hunter with his long
silver-mounted muzzle-loader, and the white profes-

sional elephant-killer with his heavy rifle. The manifestation of the glory of God was turned into an object of exploitation. Is it to be wondered at that he cannot forgive us?

Yet there is always something magnanimous about elephants. To follow a rhino in his own country is hard work; the space that he clears in the thorn-thicket is just a few inches too low for the hunter, and he will have to keep his head bent a little all the time. The elephant on his march through dense forest calmly tramples out a green fragrant tunnel, lofty like the nave of a cathedral. I once followed a herd of elephants for over a fortnight, walking in shade all the time. (In the end, unexpectedly, on the top of a very steep hill and in perfect security myself, I came upon the whole troop pacing in Indian file below me. I did not kill any of them and never saw them again.) There is a morally edifying quality as well in the very aspect of an elephant—on seeing four elephants walking together on the plain, I at once felt that I had been shown black stone sculptures of the four major Prophets. On the chessboard the elephant takes his course, irresistible, in a straight line. And the highest decoration of Denmark is the Order of the Elephant.

But a lion-hunt each single time is an affair of perfect harmony, of deep, burning, mutual desire and reverence between two truthful and undaunted creatures, on the same wave-length. A lion on the plain bears a greater likeness to ancient monumental stone lions than to the lion which to-day you see in a zoo; the sight of him goes straight to the heart. Dante cannot have been more deeply amazed and moved at the first sight of Beatrice in a street of Florence. Gazing back into the past I do, I believe, remember each individual lion I have seen—his coming into the picture, his slow raising or rapid turning of the head, the strange, snakelike swaying of his tail. "Praise be to thee, Lord, for Brother Lion, the which is very calm, with mighty paws, and flows through the flowing grass, red-mouthed, silent, with the roar of the thunder ready in his chest." And he himself, catching sight of me, may have been struck, somewhere under his royal mane, by the ring of a similar Te Deum: "Praise be to thee, Lord, for my sister of Europe, who is young, and has come out to me on the plain in the night."

In old days the lion was likely to come out of the matter triumphant. Later we have got such effective weapons that the test of strength can hardly be called fair—still I have had more than one friend killed by lions. Nowadays great sportsmen hunt with cameras. The practice started while I was still in Africa; Denys as a white hunter took out millionaires from many countries, and they brought back magnificent pictures, the which however to my mind (because I do not see eye to eye with the camera) bore less real likeness to their object than the chalk portraits drawn up on the kitchen door by our Native porters. It is a more refined sport than shooting, and provided you can make the lion join into the spirit of it you may here, at the end of a pleasant, platonic affair, without bloodshed on either side, blow one another a kiss and part like civilized beings. I have no real knowledge of the art; I was a fairly good shot with a rifle, but I cannot photograph.

When I first came out to Africa I could not live without getting a fine specimen of each single kind of African game. In my last ten years out there I did not fire a shot except in order to get meat for my Natives. It became to me an unreasonable thing, indeed in itself ugly or vulgar, for the sake of a few hours' excitement to put out a life that belonged in the great landscape and had grown up in it for ten or twenty, or—as in the

The author and her Scotch deerhound,
Dusk, in the garden at Ngong, 1919

case of buffaloes and elephants—for fifty or a hundred years. But lion-hunting was irresistible to me; I shot my last lion a short time before I left Africa.

As now on this New Year's morning as noiselessly as possible I got down from the car and, through the long wet grass that washed my hands, the rifle, and my face, slowly walked closer to the lion, he stirred, rose and stood up immovable, his shoulder towards me, as fine a target for a shot as in the course of a lifetime you would get anywhere in the world. The sun by now was just below the horizon, the morning sky behind the dark silhouette was clear like liquid gold. I was struck by a thought: "I have seen you before, I know you well. But from where?" The answer came at once: "It is a lion out of the royal coat of arms of Denmark, one of our three dark-blue lions on gold ground. *Lion posant or* it is called in the heraldic language—he knows it himself." As I sat down on the ground, got Denys' rifle into position on my knee and took aim, I made a resolution: "If I get this lion, the King of Denmark is to have the skin."

As the shot fell, booming loudly in the still morning landscape and echoing from the hills, it looked to me as if the lion was carried a couple of feet straight upwards into the air before he came down and collapsed. He had been hit in the heart, it was as it should be.

I have told in my book of how I sat and watched Denys and Kanuthia flaying the lion. Going back to that morning after so many years it seems all alive and clear round me, hard to leave once more. I knew then, without reflecting, that I was up at great height, upon the roof of the world, a small figure in the tremendous retort of earth and air, yet one with it; I did not know that I was at the height and upon the roof of my own life. The grass on the slope where I sat was short as a mowed lawn, the Masai having burned it off in patches in order to get fresh grazing for their herds, the High-land air was intoxicating, like wine, the shadows of the vultures ran across my feet. From where I sat I could gaze far away: at a very long distance, by the line of the tall acacia trees somewhat below me, three giraffes came into sight, stood still for a few minutes and walked off. "Praise be to thee, Lord, for Sister Giraffe, the which is an ambler, full of grace, exceedingly demure and absent-minded, and carries her small head high above the grass, with long lashes to her veiled eyes, and which is so much a lady that one refrains from thinking of her legs, but remembers her as floating over the plain in long garbs, draperies of morning mist or mirage."

Now it fell out that this lion was an exceptionally fine specimen, what out in his own country they call a black-maned lion, with his thick dark mane growing all back over his shoulder-blades. Denys' gun-bearer, who had seen many hundred lion-skins, declared this one to be the finest he had ever come across. And as in that same spring I was going on a visit to Denmark after four years in Africa, I took the skin with me and on my way, in London, gave it to the firm of Rowland Ward to be cured and set up.

When in Denmark I told my friends that I meant to give King Christian X the lion-skin, they laughed at me.

"It is the worst piece of snobbery that we have ever heard of," they said.

"Nay, but you do not understand," I answered them. "You have not lived for a long time outside your own country."

"But what in the world is the King to do with the skin?" they asked. "He does not mean to appear at

New Year's levee as Hercules! He will be in despair about it."

"Well," I said, "if the King will be in despair, he will have to be in despair. But I do not think it need come to that, for he will have some attic at Christiansborg or Amalienborg where he can put it away."

It so happened that Rowland Ward did not manage to have the skin ready by autumn when I was going back to Africa, so that I could not myself present it to the King, but had to leave this privilege to an old uncle of mine who was a chamberlain to the Court. If the King was really in despair about it he hid it very nobly. Some time after my return to the farm I had a kind letter from him, in which he thanked me for his lion-skin.

A letter from home always means a lot to people living for a long time out of their country. They will carry it about in their pocket for several days, to take it out from time to time and read it again. A letter from a king will mean more than other letters. I got the King's letter about Christmas-time, and I pictured to myself how the King had sat at his writing-table at Amalienborg, gazing out over a white Amalienborg Square with the snow-clad equestrian statue of his

great-great-great grandfather, King Frederic V, in a
wig and classic armour, in the midst of it. A short time
ago I myself had been part of the Copenhagen world.
I stuck the letter into the pocket of my old khaki slacks
and rode out on the farm.

The farm work that I was going to inspect was the
clearing of a square piece of woodland where we were
to plant coffee, a couple of miles from my house. I rode
through the forest, which was still fresh after the short
rains. Now once more I was part of the world of Africa.

Half an hour before I came out to the wood-fellers a
sad accident had taken place amongst them. A young
Kikuyu, whose name was Kitau, had not managed to
get away quick enough when a big tree fell, and had
had one leg crushed beneath it. I heard his long moan-
ings while still at a distance. I speeded up Rouge upon
the forest path. When I came to the place of disaster
Kitau's fellow-workers had dragged him out from beneath the fallen tree and laid him on the grass; they
were thronging round him there, separating when I
came up but standing close by to watch the effect of
the catastrophe on me and to hear what I would say
about it.

Kitau was lying in a pool of blood, his leg had been

smashed above the knee and was sticking out from his body at a grotesque and cruel angle.

I made the wood-fellers hold my horse and sent off a runner to the house to have Farah bring out the car, so that I might drive Kitau to the hospital in Nairobi. But my small Ford box-body car was getting on in years; she rarely consented to run on more than two cylinders and indeed it went against her to be started at all. With a sinking heart I realized that it would be some time before she came up.

While waiting for her I sat with Kitau. The other wood-fellers had withdrawn some distance. Kitau was in great pain, weeping all the time.

I always had morphia at hand in my house for injured people of the farm carried up there, but here I had neither the medicine nor the syringe. Kitau, when he realized that I was with him, groaned out dolefully: "*Saidea mimi*"—help me—"Msabu." And again: "*Saidea mimi*. Give me some of the medicine that helps people," the while groping over my arm and knee. When out riding on the farm I usually had bits of sugar in my pockets to give to the totos herding their goats and sheep on the plain and at the sight of me crying out for sugar. I brought out such bits and fed Kitau with them—he would or could not move his badly bruised hands, and let me place the sugar on his tongue. It was as if this medicine did somehow relieve his pain; his moans, while he had it in his mouth, changed into low whimperings. But my stock of sugar came to an end, and then once more he began to wail and writhe, long spasms ran through his body. It is a sad experience to sit by somebody suffering so direly without being able to help; you long to get up and run away or, as with a badly injured animal, to put an end to the anguish— for a moment I believe I looked round for some kind of weapon for the purpose. Then again came the repeated clock-regular moaning of Kitau: "Have you got no more, Msabu? Have you got nothing more to give me?"

In my distress I once more put my hand into my pocket and felt the King's letter. "Yes, Kitau," I said, "I have got something more. I have got something *mzuri sana*"—very excellent indeed. "I have got a *Barua a Soldani*"—a letter from a king. "And that is a thing which all people know, that a letter from a king, *mokone yake*"—in his own hand—"will do away with all pain, however bad." At that I laid the King's letter on his chest and my hand upon it. I endeavoured, I believe—out there in the forest, where Kitau and I were as if all alone—to lay the whole of my strength into it.

It was a very strange thing that almost at once the words and the gesture seemed to send an effect through him. His terribly distorted face smoothed out, he closed his eyes. After a while he again looked up at me. His eyes were so much like those of a small child that cannot yet speak that I was almost surprised when he spoke to me. "Yes," he said. "It is *mzuri*," and again, "yes, it is *mzuri sana*. Keep it there."

When at last the car arrived and we got Kitau lifted on to it, I meant to take my seat at the steering-wheel, but at that he immediately worked himself into a state of the greatest alarm. "No, Msabu," he said, "Farah can drive the car, you must tell him to do so. You will sit beside me and hold the Barua a Soldani to my stomach as before, or otherwise the bad pain will come back at once." So I sat on the boards beside him, and all the way into Nairobi held the King's letter in position. When we arrived at the hospital Kitau once more closed his eyes and kept them closed, as if refusing to take in any more impressions. But with his left hand on my clothes he kept sure that I was beside him while I parleyed with the doctor and the matron. They did indeed allow me to keep close beside him while he was laid on the stretcher, carried into the building and placed on the operating table; and as long as I saw him he was quiet.

I may in this place tell that they did really in hospital manage to set his broken leg. When he got out he could walk, even if he always limped a little.

I may also here tell that later on, in Denmark, I learned from the King himself that my lion-skin had obtained a highly honourable place in the state-room of Christiansborg Castle, with the skin of a polar bear to the other side of the throne.

But now the rumour spread amongst the squatters of my farm that I had got this Barua a Soldani, with its miracle-working power. They began to come up to my house one by one, warily, to find out more about it— the old women first, mincing about like old hens turning their heads affectedly to find a grain for their young ones. Soon they took to carrying up those of their sick who were in bad pain, so that they might have the letter laid on them and for a while be relieved. Later they wanted more. They demanded to borrow the King's letter, for the day or for the day and night, to take with them to the hut for the relief of an old dying grandmother or a small ailing child.

The Barua a Soldani amongst my stock of medicine from the very first was accurately and strictly placed in a category of its own. This decision was taken by the Natives themselves without my giving any thought to the matter. It would do away with pain, in this capacity it was infallible, and no ache or pang could hold out against it. But it must be made use of solely in uttermost need.

It did happen from time to time that a patient with a very bad toothache, in his misery cried out to me to let him have Barua a Soldani. But his appeal would be met by his surroundings with grave disapprovement and indignation or with haughty, scornful laughter. "You!" they cried back to him, "there is nothing the matter with you but that you have got a bad tooth! You can go down to old Juma Bemu and have him pull it out for you. How could you have the King's letter? Nay, but here is old Kathegu very ill in his hut with long, hard pains in his stomach, and going to die to-night. His small grandson is up here to have Barua a Soldani for him until tomorrow from Msabu. To him she will give it." By this time I had had a leather bag with a string to it made for the King's letter. So the small toto, standing up straight on the terrace, would take the remedy carefully from my hands, hang it round his neck and walk away, with his own hands upon it. He would stand up straight on the terrace again next morning. Ay, his grandfather had died at sunrise, but Burua a Soldani had helped him well all night.

I have seen this particular attitude, or this particular mentality, in the dark people in other matters as well. They stood in a particular relation to the ways and conditions of life. There are things which can be done and others which cannot be done, and they fell in with the law, accepting what came with a kind of aloof humility—or pride.

When Fathima, Farah's wife, was to give birth to her first child, she was very ill; for an hour or two her surroundings, and her mother herself, had given up hope about her. Her mother, an imposing figure in my establishment, had arranged for about a dozen Somali ladies of the first families of Nairobi to be present. They arrived in Aly Khan's mule-traps, looking very lovely and lively, like old Persian pictures, in their long ample skirts and veils, and filled with sympathy and zeal. The waves of woman's world closed over Farah's house, at some distance from the huts of my house-boys. Farah himself, grave and more subdued than I had ever seen him, together with all other male creatures of my household, had been shooed a hundred yards away. The women then set to heating up the room in which the birth was taking place, to an almost unbearable heat, with charcoal in basins, and to make the air thick with childbed-incense. I sat out there for a while, half unconscious, not because I imagined that I could be of any use whatever, but because I felt it to be the correct thing and expected of me.

Fathima was a very lovely creature, with big dark eyes like a doe's, so slim that one wondered where she could possibly be storing her baby, supple in all her movements and in daily life of a risible temper. I felt sorry for her now. The gentle midwives were busy, bending and again straightening up the girl and from time to time knocking her in the small of the back with their fists as if to knock out the child. For the time that I was there I saw them dealing out only one kind of medicine: a matron amongst them brought along an earthenware dish, on the inner side of which a holy man of the town had drawn up, in charcoal, a text from the Koran; the lettering was washed off carefully with water, and the water poured into the mouth of the labouring young woman.

This great event on the farm took place at the time when the Prince of Wales—the present Duke of Windsor—was on his first visit to the country. Among the celebrations in his honour was a *concours hippique* in Nairobi, and I had entered my Irish pony Poor-Box for the jumping competition—he was at the moment in training at Limoru. In the midst of the bustle round me and in a moment of things' looking very dark, I suddenly called to mind that I had promised to bring over a bag of oats for him there, so I would have to leave for a couple of hours. I drove away sadly, taking Kamante with me in the car.

On the way back from Limoru I came past the French Mission and remembered that the Fathers for some time had been promising me seed of a particular kind of lettuce from France. As I pulled up the car, Kamante, who during our drive had not said a word, spoke to me. Fathima was a favourite with Kamante, she was the only human being for whose intelligence I had ever heard him express any kind of respect. "Are you," he asked me, "going into the church to beg the lady in there, who is your friend, to help Fathima?" The lady in the church, who was my friend, was the Virgin Mary, whose statue Kamante had seen when on Christmas night he had accompanied me to midnight mass. I could not very well say no, so I answered yes, and went into the church before going to the refectory. It was cool in the church, and in the face of the highly vulgar papier mâché statue of the Virgin, with a lily in her hand, there was something soothing and hopeful.

When I came back to my house, Fathima's baby was born, and she herself was doing well. I congratulated her mother and Farah in his forest exile. The small boy brought into the world that day was Ahamed, called Saufe, who later became a great figure on the farm. Kamante said to me: "You see, Msabu, it was good that I reminded you to ask the lady who is your friend to help Fathima."

Now, one would have imagined that with knowledge of my intimacy with a person of such power, Kamante upon some other occasion would have come back to have me make use of it. But this never happened. There are things which can be done, and other things which cannot be done. And we who know the laws must fall in with them.

In the course of time, however, my squatters tried to find out more about that King of my own country who had written the letter. They asked me if he was tall, and were here, I believe, still under the impression of the personality of the Prince of Wales, who had dined on the farm, and who had made them wonder at the fact that a person of such great might should be so slim and slight. I was pleased to be able to reply truthfully that there was not a taller man in his kingdom. They then wanted to know whether the horse on which he rode was more *kali*—fierce—than my own horse, Rouge; then again, if he laughed. This last must have been a matter of importance to the Natives in their relations with us. "Your *kabilla*"—tribe—they said to me, "is different to those of the other white people. You do not get angry with us as they do. You laugh at us."

I have still got the King's letter. But it is now un-decipherable, brown and stiff with blood and matter of long ago.

In a showcase at the Museum of Rosenborg, in Co-penhagen, the tourist can see a piece of yellow texture covered with tawny spots. It is the handkerchief of King Christian IV, which the King held to his eye socket when, in the naval battle of Kolberger Heide three hun-dred years ago, his eye was smashed by a Swedish shot. A Danish poet of the last century has written an enthu-siastic ode about these proud, edifying marks.

The blood on my sheet of paper is not proud or edify-ing. It is the blood of a dumb nation. But then the hand-writing on it is that of a king, *mokone yake*. No ode will be written about my letter; still, today it is, I believe, history as much as the relic of Rosenborg. Within it, in paper and blood, a covenant has been signed between the Europeans and the Africans—no similar document of this same relationship is likely to be drawn up again.

The Great Gesture

I was a fairly famous doctor to the squatters of the farm, and it happened that patients came down from Limoru or Kijabe to consult me. I had been, in the beginning of my career, miraculously lucky in a few cures, which had made my name echo in the manyattas. Later I had made some very grave mistakes, of which I still cannot think without dismay, but they did not seem to affect my prestige; at times I felt that the people liked me better for not being infallible. This trait in the Africans comes out in other of their relations with the Europeans.

My consultation hour was vaguely from nine to ten,

my consultation room the stone-paved terrace east of my house.

On most days my activity was limited to driving in the sick people to the hospital in Nairobi or up to that of the Scotch Mission at Kikuyu, both of which were good hospitals. There would almost always be plague about somewhere in the district; with this you were bound to take the sufferers to Nairobi plague hospital, or your farm would be put in quarantine. I was not afraid of plague, since I had been told that one would either die from the disease or rise from it as fit as ever, and since, besides, I felt that it would be a noble thing to die from an illness to which popes and queens had succumbed. There would likewise almost always be smallpox about, and gazing at old and young faces round me, stamped for life like thimbles, I was afraid of smallpox, but Government regulations strictly kept us to frequent inoculations against the illness. As to other diseases like meningitis or typhoid fever, whether I drove the patients into Nairobi or tried to cure them myself out on the farm, I was always convinced that I should not catch the sickness—my faith may have been due to an instinct, or may have been in itself a kind of protection. The first *sais* that I had on the farm, Malindi—who was a dwarf, but a great man with horses—died from meningitis actually in my arms.

Most of my own practice was thus concerned with the lighter accidents of the place—broken limbs, cuts, bruises and burns—or with coughs, children's diseases and eye diseases. At the start I knew but little above what one is taught at a first-aid course. My later skill was mostly obtained through experiments on my patients, for a doctor's calling is demoralizing. I arrived at setting a broken arm or ankle with a splint, advised all through the operation by the sufferer himself, who very likely might have performed it on his own, but who took pleasure in setting me to work. Ambition a few times made me try my hand at undertakings which later I had to drop again. I much wanted to give my patients Salvarsan—which in those days was a fairly new medicine and was given in big doses—but although my hand was steady with a rifle I was nervous about it with a syringe for intravenous injections. Dysentery I could generally keep in check with small, often-repeated doses of Epsom salt, and malaria with quinine. Yet it was in connection with a case of malaria that I was nearest to becoming a murderer.

On a day in the beginning of the long rains Berkeley

Cole came round the farm from up-country, on his way to Nairobi. A little while after, Juma appeared to report that an old Masai Chief with his followers was outside, asking for medicine for a son of his who had been taken ill, evidently—from the symptoms reported—with malaria.

The Masai were my neighbours; if I rode across the river which formed the border of my farm I was in their Reserve. But the Masai themselves were not always there. They trekked with their big herds of cattle from one part of the grass-land—which was about the size of Ireland—to another, according to the rains and the condition of the grazing. When again they came round my way and set to patch up their huts of cow-hide for a sojourn of some time, they would send over to notify me, and I would ride over to call on them.

If I had been alone this afternoon, I should have gone outside to talk the case over with the old Chief, to hand him the quinine and altogether to get Masai news. But Berkeley, dried after his drive and revived by a glass or two, was in one of his sweet, dazzling moods and entertaining me on old Ireland memories of his, so that I sat on with him. I just handed over the keys of the medicine

chest to Kamante, who was the skilled and deep amanuensis to my doctor and had dealt out quinine to our patients a hundred times, telling him to count up the tab-
lets to the father of the sick boy and to instruct him to
give his son two of them in the evening and six in the
course of the next day. But after dinner, while Berkeley
and I by the fireside were listening to my records of
Petrouchka just out from Europe, Juma once more stood
in the door, an ominous spectre in his long white *kansu*,
to inform me that the old Masai was back with a small
lot of his people. For his son, after having taken my medicine, had got very ill indeed, with terrible pains in his
stomach. I called in the Masai Chief, and found that he
was an old acquaintance of mine. I knew his son well
too, his name was Sandoa; like the big Masai Chief, he
was a Moran of two years ago, and it was he who had
taught me to shoot with a bow and arrow. Calling to
mind that the most inexplicable fits of idiocy might
occur even in the most intelligent Natives, I had Kamante woken up and ordered him to show me the box
from which he had taken the quinine. And it was Lysol.

Berkeley said: "We had better go out there at once."
But it was raining heavily; the road round Mbagathi

Bridge was impassable, so that it would be useless to think of starting a car, and we should have to take the shorter cut across the river on foot. I collected the bicarbonate and oil which I used against accidents with corrosives, and we took two boys with hurricane lamps with us. The Masai also had brought lamps. The descent to the river, in the tall wet bush and long wet grass, was steep and stony, but the Masai knew of a better way than my riding-path, and when we came to the river itself, which had swelled high with the rain, they carried me across.

On the way none of us had spoken. As now, to the other side of the river, we were ascending the long slope of the Masai Reserve, I said to Berkeley: "If Sandoa is dead by the time we get there, I shall not go back to the farm. I shall stay on with the Masai. If they will have me." I had no answer from Berkeley, only, the next moment, a sudden, wild, extremely rude curse straight in my face. For he had in that second put his foot into the long marching column of an army of Siafu. The Siafu are the universally dreaded, man-eating ants of Africa, the which, left to themselves, will eat you up alive. My dogs in their hut at night when they had got the Siafu on them would yell out miserably in their agony, until you rushed out to save them. My friend Ingrid Lindström of Njoro at one time had her whole flock of turkeys devoured by the killers. They are about mostly at night, and in the rainy season. If you happen to get the Siafu on you, there is nothing for you but to tear off your clothes and have the person nearest at hand pluck them out of your flesh. Now, turning round to see what was happening to Berkeley, I saw him, in the midst of the infinite black African night and of the Masai plain, his trousers at his heels, changing feet as if he were treading water, with one toto holding up a hurricane lamp and another picking out the burning, ferocious creatures from his strangely white legs.

When we came to the Masai manyatta we found Sandoa still alive. By a stroke of luck, or by some kind of intuition, he had taken but one tablet of Kamante's medicine—possibly also the intestines of Masai Morani are hardier than those of other human beings. I administered the bicarbonate and oil to him, feeling that I ought to be on my knees with gratitude, and I saw him well on his way to recovery before, in the grey light of dawn, Berkeley and I returned to my house.

Snake-bites were frequent, but although I lost oxen and dogs from snake-bite I never lost a human patient from them. The spitting cobra caused pain and distress; I still have before me the picture of an old squatter woman staggering up to the house wailing and blind after having her face spat in while cutting wood in the forest—she must have been chopping with her mouth wide open, for her tongue and gums were swollen to suffocation and had turned a deadly pale blue. But the effect of the poison could be relieved with bicarbonate and oil and would pass after a while.

Fashion—the ambition to be *comme il faut*—made itself felt in the ailments on the farm, as in other departments of Native life. At one time the truly chic thing was to come to the house for worm-medicine. I did not myself taste the mixture, which looked very nasty in its bottle, like green slime, but the people, old and young, drank it down with pride. After a while I warned my patients that I had no faith in their need of worm-medicine, and that if they wanted to go on taking it as an apéritif they would in the future have to pay for it themselves—and I thereby put an end to that particular kind of dandyism. A very old squatter a couple of years later

Aweru, an old Kikuyu squatter of the farm

presented himself at the house and begged to have the "green medicine." His wife, he informed me, had got a *nyoka*—which word really means a snake—in her stomach, and at night it would roar so loudly that neither he nor she could sleep. On my doorstep he looked *démodé,* the last adherent to a fashion of the past.

My patients and I thus worked together in good understanding. Only one shadow lay over the terrace: that of the hospital. During my early days in Africa, till the end of the First World War, the shadow was light like that of trees in spring; later on it grew and darkened.

For some of my years on the farm I had been holding the office of *fermier général* there—that is, in order to save the Government trouble I collected the taxes from my squatters locally and sent in the sum total to Nairobi. In this capacity I had many times had to listen to the Kikuyu complaining that they were made to pay up their money for things which they would rather have done without: roads, railways, street lighting, police— and hospitals.

I wished to understand them and to know how deep was their reluctance against the hospital, and to what it was really due, but it was not easy, for they would not let me know; they closed up when I questioned them, they died before my eyes, as Africans will. One must wait and be patient in order to find the right moment for putting salt on the tail of the timid, dark birds.

It fell to Sirunga, in one of his little quicksilver movements, to give me a kind of information.

Sirunga was one of the many grandchildren of my big squatter Kaninu, but his father was a Masai. His mother had been among those pretty young girls whom Kaninu had sold across the river, but she had come back again to her father's land with her baby son. He was a small, slightly built child with a sudden, wild, flying gracefulness in all his movements and a corresponding, incalculable, crazy imagination of a kind which I have not met in any other Native child, and which maybe will have been due to the mixture of blood. The other boys kept back from Sirunga, they called him "*Sheitani*" —the Devil—and at first I laughed at it—for even with a good deal of mischief in him Sirunga could be nothing but a very small devil—but later on I realized that in the boys' eyes he was possessed by the Devil, and his smallness then made the fact the more tragic. Sirunga suffered from epilepsy.

I did not know of it until I happened to see him under an attack. I was lying on the lawn in front of the house talking with him and some other totos when all at once he rose up straight and announced: *"Na taka kufa"*— I am dying, or literally, I want to die, as they say in Swahili. His face grew very still, the mouth so patient. The boys round him at once spread to all sides. The attack, when it came upon him, was indeed terrible to watch, he stiffened in cramp and foamed from the mouth. I sat with my arms round him; I had never till then seen an epileptic attack and did not know what to do about it. Sirunga's amazement as he woke up in my arms was very deep, he was used to seeing everybody run away when he was seized with a fit, and his dark gaze at my face was almost hostile. All the same after this he kept close to me—I have before written about him that he held the office of an inventive fool or jester and followed me everywhere like a small, fidgety, black shadow. His mighty uncontrolled fantasies and whims were totally confused and highly confusing to listen to. Sirunga, at a time when we had an epidemic on the farm, explained to me that once—long long long ago—all people had been very ill. It was, Msabu, when the sun was pregnant with the moon—walked with the moon in the stomach—but as the moon jumped out and was born, they grew well again. I did not connect his fantasy with hospitals, from which no such universal cure could rightly be expected; it was the words "long long long ago" which gave me my perspective.

At the time when the Natives of the Highlands were free to die as they liked, they would follow the ways of their fathers and mothers. When a Kikuyu fell ill, his people carried him out of his hut on his bedstead of sticks and hides, since a hut in which a person had died must not again be lived in but had to be burned down. Out here under the tall fringed trees his family sat round him and kept him company, squatter friends came up to give the news and gossip of the farm, at night small charcoal fires were made up on the ground round the bed. If the sick man got well he was carried back into the hut. If he died he was brought across the river out on the plain, and was left there to the quick and neat cleaning and polishing of jackals and vultures, and of the lions coming down from the hills.

I myself was in sympathy with the tradition of the Natives, and I instructed Farah—who showed himself deeply averse to the idea, for the Mohammedans wall up the graves of their dead and perform solemn rites by the side of them—if I died on the farm to let me travel in the track of my old squatters across the river. There were so many of the true qualities of the Highland country in the *castrum doloris* out there under the big firmament, with its wild, free, gluttonous undertakers: silent drama, a kind of silent fun—at which after a day or two the main character himself would be smiling— and silent nobility. The silent, all-embracing genius of consent.

The Government prohibited and put an end to the funeral custom of old days, and the Natives gave it up unwillingly. The Government and the Missions then undertook to build hospitals, and, seeing the reluctance of the people of the land to go into them, were surprised and indignant, and blamed them for being ungrateful and superstitious, or for being cowards.

The Africans, though, feared pain or death less than we ourselves did, and life having taught them the uncertainty of all things, they were at any time ready to take a risk. An old man with a headache once asked me if I might not be able to cut off his head, take out the evil

from it, and set it back in its right place, and if I had
consented I think that he would have let me make the
experiment. It was other things in us which at times set
their nerves on edge.

For they had had our civilization presented to them
piecemeal, like incoherent parts of a mechanism which
they had never seen functioning, and the functioning of
which they could not on their own imagine. We had
been transforming, to them, Rite into Routine. What by
now most of all they feared from our hands was boredom, and on being taken into hospital they may well
have felt that they were in good earnest being taken
in to die from boredom.

They had deep roots to their nature as well, down in
the soil and back in the past, the which, like all roots,
demanded darkness. When, in his small confused Ki-
kuyu-Masai mind, Sirunga had given me a small con-
torted key, the reference to a past—"long long long ago"
—an African past of a thousand years, I took it into my
course of thought. We white people, I reflected, were
wrong when in our intercourse with the people of the
ancient continent we forgot or ignored their past or did
indeed decline to acknowledge that they had ever

existed before their meeting with us. We had deliber-
ately deprived our picture of them of a dimension, thus
allowing it to become distorted to our eyes and blurred
in its Native harmony and dignity, and our error of vision had caused deep and sad misunderstandings between us and them. The view to me later on was con-
firmed as I observed the fact that white people to whom
the past was still a reality—in whose minds the past of
their country, their name and blood or their home was
naturally alive—would get on easier with the Africans
and would come closer to them than others, to whom
the world was created yesterday, or upon the day when
they got their new car.

The dark people, then, as the clever doctor from Volaia approached, may well have gone through the kind
of agony which one will imagine a tree to be suffering at
the approach of a zealous forester intending to pull up
her roots for inspection. Their hearts in an instinctive
deadly nausea turned from the medical examinations of
the hospitals, such as they did from the *kipanda,* the
passport giving the name and data of its bearer, which
some years later the Government made compulsory to
each individual Native of the Highlands.

We Nations of Europe, I thought, who do not fear to floodlight our own inmost mechanisms, are here turning the blazing lights of our civilization into dark eyes, fitly set like the eyes of doves by the rivers of waters (Song of Solomon 5:12), essentially different to ours. If for a long enough time we continue in this way to dazzle and blind the Africans, we may in the end bring upon them a longing for darkness, which will drive them into the gorges of their own, unknown mountains and their own, unknown minds.

We may, if we choose to, I thought further, look forward to the day when we shall have convinced them that it be a meritorious and happy undertaking to floodlight a whole continent. But for that they will have to get other eyes. The intelligent, efficient and base Swahili of the coast have got such eyes.

The outcome of these various circumstances was this: that I would from time to time find myself unemployed as a doctor, and my consulting room empty.

It would most often happen after I had been taking a patient into hospital. But it might be brought about, suddenly, by reasons unknown to me and probably unknowable, like the sudden pause which may occur amongst labourers in the field. They would then, after a week, bring me up a patient or two with a high fever or a broken limb, too far gone for treatment. I would feel that I was being made a fool of, and lose patience with my people, I would speak to them without mercy:

"Why," I asked them, "must you wait to come to me with your broken arms and legs until they are gangrenous, and the stench, as I am driving you to Nairobi, makes me myself sick?—or with a festering eye until the ball of it has shrunk and withered so that the cleverest doctor of Volaia will not be able to cure it? The old fat Msabu matron in the Nairobi hospital will be angry with me once more and will tell me that I do not mind whether my people on the farm live or die—and in the future she shall be right. You are more obstinate than your own goats and sheep, and I am tired of working for you, and from now on I shall bandage and dose your goats and sheep and leave you yourself to be one-legged and one-eyed, such as you choose to be."

Upon this they would stand for some time without a word, and then, very sullenly, let me know that they would in the future bring me up their injuries in good time, if on my side I would promise not to take them into hospital.

During the last few months that I was still on the farm, at the time when very slowly it was being made clear to me that my fight of many years was lost, and that I should have to leave my life in Africa and go home to Europe, I had as a patient a small boy of six or seven named Wawerru, who had got bad burns on both legs. Burns are an ailment which you would often get to treat in the Kikuyu, for they built up piles of charcoal in their huts and slept round them, and it happened that in the course of the night the coals slid down on top of the sleepers.

In the midst of a strangely non-real existence, unconnected with past or future, the moments that I spent in doctoring Wawerru were sweet to me, like a breeze on a parched plain. The French Fathers had presented me with a new kind of ointment for burns, just out from France. Wawerru was a slight, slant-eyed child, late-born in his family and spoilt, in so far as he believed that nobody would do him anything but good. He or his elder brothers who carried him up to the house had managed to grasp the idea of a treatment every third day, and his sores were yielding to my cure. Kamante as my amanuensis was aware of the happiness that the task gave me, his lynx eyes every third day would seek out the small group amongst the patients on the terrace, and one time, when they had missed a day, he gave himself the trouble to walk down to Wawerru's manyatta and to admonish his family about their duties. Then suddenly Wawerru did not appear, he vanished out of my existence. I questioned another toto about him; "*Sejui*"—I know not—he answered. A few days later I rode down to the manyatta, my dogs running with me.

The manyatta lay at the foot of a long, green grass-slope. It contained a large number of huts, for Wawerru's father had got several wives, with a hut to each of them and—in the way of most wealthy Kikuyu—a central hut of his own, into which he could retire from the world of femininity to meditate in peace, and there was also an irregular suburb of bigger and smaller granaries to the settlement.

As I rode down the slope, I saw Wawerru himself sitting on the grass, playing with a couple of other totos. One of his play-fellows caught sight of me and notified him, and he at once, without so much as a glance in my direction, set off into the maze of the huts and disappeared to my eyes. His legs were still too weak to carry him, he scuttled along with wondrous quickness on all fours like a mouse. I quite suddenly was thrown into a state of flaming anger at the sight of such ingratitude. I set Rouge into a canter to catch up with him, and at the moment when, in the exact way of a mouse with its hole, he slipped into a hut, I jumped from the saddle and followed him. Rouge was a wise horse; if I left him, the reins loose round his neck, he would stand still and wait for me till I came back. I had my riding whip in my hand.

The hut to my eyes, as I came into it from the sunlight of the plain, was almost dark; there were a few dim figures in it, old men or women. Wawerru, when he realized that he had been run to earth, without a sound rolled over on his face. Then I saw that the long bandages, with which I had taken so much trouble, had been unwound, and that from heel to hip his legs were smeared with a thick coat of cow-dung. Now cow-dung is not actually a bad remedy for burns, since it coagulates quickly and will keep the air out. But at the mo-

ment the sight and smell of it to me were nauseating, as
if deadly—in a kind of self-preservation I tightened my
grip on the whip.

I had not, till now, in my mind associated my success
or failure in curing Wawerru's legs with my own fate, or
with the fate of the farm. Standing here in the hut, ad-
justing my eyes to the twilight of it, I saw the two as one,
and the world round me grew infinitely cheerless, a
place of no hope. I had ventured to believe that efforts
of mine might defeat destiny. It was brought home to
me now how deeply I had been mistaken; the balance-
sheet was laid before me, and proved that whatever I
took on was destined to end up in failure. Cow-dung
was to be my harvest. I bethought myself of the old
Jacobite song:

> *Now all is done that could be done.*
> *And all is done in vain.*

I spoke no word, I do not think that I gave out any
sound at all. But the tears all at once welled out from
behind my eyelids, and I could not stop them. In a few
moments I felt my face bathed in tears. I kept standing
like that for what seemed to me a long time, and the si-

lence of the hut to me was deep. Then, as the situation had to end somehow, I turned and went out, and my tears still flowed abundantly, so that twice I missed the door. Outside the hut I found Rouge waiting; I got into the saddle and rode away slowly.

When I had ridden ten yards, I turned round to look for my dogs. I then saw that a number of people had come out from the huts and were gazing after me. Riding on another ten or twenty yards, I was struck by the thought that this in my squatters was an unusual behaviour. In general, unless they wanted something from me and would shout for it—as the totos, popping from the long grass, screeched out for sugar—or wanted just to send off a friendly greeting: "Jambu, Msabu!" they let me pass fairly unnoticed. I turned round again to have another look at them. This second time there were still more people standing on the grass, immovable, following me with their eyes. Indeed the whole population of the manyatta would have got on their legs to watch Rouge and me slowly disappearing across the plain. I thought: "They have never till now seen me cry. Maybe they have not believed that a white person ever did cry. I ought not to have done it."

The dogs, having finished their investigation of the various scents of the manyatta and their chasing of its hens, were coming with me. We went home together.

Early next morning, before Juma had come in to draw the curtains of my windows, I sensed, by the intensity of the silence round me, that a crowd was gathered at short distance. I had had the same experience before and have written about it. The Africans have got this to them —they will make their presence known by other means than eyesight, hearing or smell, so that you do not tell yourself: "I see them," "I hear them," or "I smell them," but: "They are here." Wild animals have got the same quality, but our domestic animals have lost it.

"They have come up here, then," I reflected. "What are they bringing me?" I got up and went out.

There were indeed a great many people on the terrace. As I kept standing silent, looking at them, they, silent too, formed a circle round me; they obviously would not have let me go away had I wanted to. There were old men and women here, mothers with babies on their back, impudent Morani, coy Nditos—maidens—and lively, bright-eyed totos. Gazing from one face to another I realized what in our daily life together I never thought of: that they were dark, so much darker than I. Slowly they thronged closer to me.

Confronted with this kind of dumb, deadly determination in the African, a European in his mind will grope for words in which to formulate and fix it—in the same way as that in which, in the fairy-tale, the man pitting his strength against the troll must find out the name of his adversary and pin him down to a word, or be in a dark, trollish manner, lost. For a second my mind, running wildly, responded to the situation in a wild question: "Do they mean to kill me?" The moment after I struck on the right formula. My people of the farm had come up to tell me: "The time has come." "It has, I see," in my mind I assented. "But the time for what?"

An old woman was the first to open her mouth to me.

The old women of the farm were all good friends of mine. I saw less of them than of the small restless totos, who were ever about my house, but they had agreed to assume the existence of a particular understanding and intimacy between them and me, as if they had all been aunties of mine. Kikuyu women with age shrink and grow darker; seen beside the cinnamon-coloured Nditos, sap-filled, sleek lianas of the forest, they look like sticks of charcoal, weightless, desiccated all through, with a kind of grim jocosity at the core of them, noble, high-class achievements of the skilled charcoal-burner of existence.

This old woman of the terrace now, in the grip of her left hand, held forth her right hand to me, as if she were making me a present of it. Across the wrist ran a scarlet burn. "Msabu," she whimpered into my face. "I have got a sick hand, sick. It needs medicine." The burn was but superficial.

An old man with a cut in the leg from his wood-chopper's axe came up next, then a couple of mothers with feverish babies, then a Moran with a split lip and another with a sprained ankle, and an Ndito with a bruise in one round breast. None of the injuries were serious. I was even pressed upon to examine a collection of splinters in the palm of a hand, from a climb for honey in a tree.

Slowly I took in the situation. My people of the farm, I realized, today, in a common great resolution had agreed to bring me what, against all reason and against the inclination of their own hearts, I had wanted from them. They must have been grappling with, imparting to one another and discussing between them the fact: "We have been trying her too hard. She clearly is unable to bear any more. The time has come to indulge her."

It could not be explained away that I was being made a fool of. But I was being made so with much generosity.

After a minute or two I could not help laughing. And as, scrutinizing my face, they caught the change in it, they joined me. One after another all faces round me lightened up and broke in laughter. In the faces of toothless old women a hundred delicate wrinkles screwed up cheeks and chin into a baroque, beaming mask—and they were no longer scars left by the warfare of life, but the traces of many laughters.

The merriment ran along the terrace and spread to the edge of it like ripples on water. There are few things in life as sweet as this suddenly rising, clear tide of African laughter surrounding one.

*Legend has it that a Gaul
seeing wild, fierce Gallic courage
mowed down round him by the rigid
discipline of Roman legions,*

heavenwards shot his last arrow,
at the God whom he had worshipped,
at the God who had betrayed him.
And then fell with cloven forehead.

From the bones of fallen Gauls
peasants of the land built fences
round their fair and fruitful vineyards.
No one had a nobler burial.

Echoes from the Hills

I have the great good luck in life that when I sleep I dream, and my dreams are always beautiful. The nightmare, with its squint-eyed combination of claustrophobia and *horror vacui,* I know from other people's accounts only, and mostly, for the last twenty years, from books and theatre. This gift of dreaming runs in my family, it is highly valued by all of us and makes us feel that we have been favoured above other human beings. An old aunt of mine asked to have written on her tombstone: "She saw many a hard day. But her nights were sweet."

But our beautiful dreams are not confined to the spheres of the idyll or the child's play, or to any such sphere as in the life of day-time is considered safe or pleasant. Horrible events take place in them, monsters appear, abysses open, wild turbulent flights and pursuits are familiar features of theirs. Only, on entering their world, horror changes hue. Monstrosity and monsters, Hell itself—they turn to favour and to prettiness.

I have read or been told that in a book of etiquette of the seventeenth century the very first rule forbids you to tell your dreams to other people, since they cannot possibly be of interest to them. I do not want to sin against seventeenth-century good manners and am not, here, going to report to my readers any particular dream of mine. But since dreams in general to me are a matter of interest, I shall set down a few general remarks about them. Should these remarks turn out somewhat vague and hazy, as if shimmering to the eyes, the reader will have to forbear with me. It is in the nature of things. Dreams, like smells, decline to yield up their inmost being to words.

The first characteristic of my dreams is this: I move in a world deeply and sweetly familiar to me, a world which belongs to me and to which I myself belong more intensely than is ever the case in my waking existence. Yet I do not in the dream meet anybody or anything which, outside of it, I know or have ever known. It has happened to me, as a child, to dream of a particularly dear dog—then I at once realized that Natty Bumppo had gone from the world of the living—but otherwise those cherished places within, or towards, which I travel, those friends, infinitely dear to my heart, whom I am rushing forward to meet and from whom I cannot bear to part, I have never seen.

Only during one time of my life, and only in connection with one kind of places and people, have phenomena of an outer world found their way into my dreams. It was in itself to me a strange and stirring experience.

The second characteristic of my dreams is their vastness, their quality of infinite space. I move in mighty landscapes, among tremendous heights, depths and expanses and with unlimited views to all sides. The loftiness and airiness of the dream come out again in its colour scheme of rare, luminous blues and violets, and mystically transparent browns—all of which I promise myself to remember in the day-time, yet there can never recall. Dream trees are very much taller than day-time trees; I vow to myself to keep in mind that such be the real height of trees, yet when I wake up I fail to do so. Long perspectives stretch before me, distance is the password of the scenery, at times I feel that the fourth dimension is within reach. I fly, in dream, to any altitude, I dive into bottomless, clear, bottle-green waters. It is a weightless world. Its very atmosphere is joy, its crowning happiness, unreasonably or against reason, is that of triumph.

For we have in the dream forsaken our allegiance to the organizing, controlling and rectifying forces of the world, the Universal Conscience. We have sworn fealty to the wild, incalculable, creative forces, the Imagination of the Universe.

To the Conscience of the world we may address ourselves in prayer, it will faithfully reward its faithful servants according to their desert, and its highest award is peace of mind.

To the imagination of the world we do not pray. We call to mind how, when last we did so, we were asked back, quick as lightning, where we had been when the morning stars sang together, or whether we could bind the sweet influences of Pleiades. Without our having asked them for freedom, these free forces have set us free as mountain winds, have liberated us from initiative and determination, as from responsibility. They deal out no wages, each of their boons to us is a gift, baksheesh, and their highest gift is inspiration. A gift may be named after both the giver and the receiver, and in this way my inspiration is my own, more even than anything else I possess, and is still the gift of God.

The ship has given up tacking and has allied herself to the wind and the current; now her sails fill and she runs on, proudly, upon obliging waves. Is her speed her own achievement and merit or the work and merit of outside powers? We cannot tell. The dancer in the waltz gives herself into the hands of her skilled partner; is the flight and wonder of the dance, now, her own achievement or his? Neither the ship nor the dancer, nor the dreamer, will be able to answer or will care to answer. But they will, all three, have experienced the supreme triumph of Unconditional Surrender.

One last word about dreams:

Some people tell me that the capacity of dreaming

belongs to childhood and early youth, and that as your faculties of seeing and hearing ebb away your talent for dreaming will go with them. My own experience tells me that it is the other way. I dream today more than I ever did as a child or a young girl, and in my present dreams things stand out more clearly than ever, and more to be wondered at.

At times I believe that my feet have been set upon a road which I shall go on following, and that slowly the centre of gravity of my being will shift over from the world of day, from the domain of organizing and regulating universal powers, into the world of Imagination. Already now I feel, as when at the age of twenty I was going to a ball in the evening, that day is a space of time without meaning, and that it is with the coming of dusk, with the lighting of the first star and the first candle, that things will become what they really are, and will come forth to meet me.

The unruly river, which has bounced along wildly, sung out loudly and raged against her banks, will widen and calm down, will in the end fall silently into the ocean of dreams, and silently experience the supreme triumph of Unconditional Surrender.

During my first months after my return to Denmark from Africa, I had great trouble in seeing anything at all as reality.

My African existence had sunk below the horizon, the Southern Cross for a short while stood out after it, like a luminous track in the sky, then faded and disappeared. The landscapes, the beasts and the human beings of that existence could not possibly mean more to my surroundings in Denmark than did the landscapes, beasts and human beings of my dreams at night. Their names here were just words, the name of Ngong was an address. It was no good, it might even be bad manners, to talk about them.

Fate had willed it that my visitors to the farm by that time had already gone, or were just about to go. They were none of them people to stay for a long time in the same place. Sir Northrop MacMillan, Galbraith and Berkeley Cole and Denys Finch-Hatton had set out before myself; shortly after my departure Lord Delamere, Lord Francis Scott and Hugh Martin followed them. The Swede, Eric von Otter, who had distinguished himself in the war in Africa, died in his faraway post up north, my gallant young friend and helpmate, Gustav

Mohr, was drowned ferrying his safari across a river. There they were, all of them, nine thousand feet up, safe in the mould of Africa, slowly being turned into African mould themselves. And here was I, walking in the fair woods of Denmark, listening to the waves of Öresund. To the southeast, a long way off, the plains of the farm, where in years of drought we had fought the wild, gluttonous grass-fires, and the squatters' plots, with the pigeons cooing high about the chattering and the sounds of cooking below, were being cut up into residential plots for Nairobi business people, and the lawns, across which I had seen the zebras galloping, were laid out into tennis courts. These things were what are called facts, but were difficult to retain.

What business had I had ever to set my heart on Africa? The old continent had done well before my giving it a thought; might it not have gone on doing so? As I myself could not find the answer, a great master supplied it. He said: "What is Africa to you or you to Africa . . . ?" And again, laughing:

> *If it do come to pass*
> *That any man turn ass,*

Leaving his wealth and ease,
A stubborn will to please,
Ducdame . . .
Here shall he see
Gross fools as he,
An if he will come to me.

Dear Master, you have never failed me, your word has been a lamp unto my feet and a light unto my path. Now I shall tell you, and prove to you, how right you have been in speaking about the stubborn will.

For a while, after I had published my book *Seven Gothic Tales*, I considered the possibility of running a children's hospital in the Masai Reserve. There was much disease among the Masai, mostly such as we had brought upon them; on my safaris I had seen many blind children. But the Masai refused to take their sick to hospital.

The Masai did not like us and had no reason to do so. For we had put an end to their bird-of-prey raids on the agricultural tribes, we had taken their spears and their big almond-shaped shields from them, and had splashed a bucket of water upon the halo of a warrior nation,

hardened through a thousand years into a personifica-
tion of that ideal of Nietzsche: "Man for war, and
woman for the warrior's delight, all else is foolishness."

Once when I was on safari deep in the Reserve, a very
old Masai came up and seated himself by my campfire;
after a while he began to speak, and it was like hearing
a boulder speak. I myself spoke sufficient Masai to enquire about game and water, and no more. For it is to
my mind a language impossible to learn, maybe because
the course of thought of the tribe speaking it is alien to
our own. When on a path in the Reserve you meet a
Masai you greet him: "Saubaa." If you meet a Masai
woman you salute her: "Tarquenya." I have never succeeded in learning what was the meaning of the difference. But on my safaris I had an interpreter with me.
"Nowadays," according to him, the Moran—warrior—of
sixty years ago told us, "it is no pleasure to live. But in
the old days it was good fun. When then the Kikuyu or
the Wakamba had got a fat piece of land, and fat herds
of cattle, goats and sheep on it, we Morani came to
them. First we killed all men and male children with
steel"—the Masai warriors had long, fine spears and
short, strong swords—"and we were allowed to stay on

in the village until we had eaten up the sheep and goats there. Then before going away again, we killed off the women with wood"—for the Masai also in their belts carried wooden clubs, surprisingly light and effective. I do not know if our old guest was actually calling up a past, or if in his long nocturnal monologue he was picturing to himself an ideal state of things, and was slowly getting drunk on his vision of it. He walked away at last and disappeared into the night, a bald, skinny bird of prey of a dying species.

Neither did the white settlers in general like the Masai, who refused to work for them and kept up a sullen and arrogant manner in their dealings with them. But I myself had always been on friendly terms with my neighbours of the Masai Reserve, and they might, I felt, consent to bring their sick children to a nursing home of mine. I travelled to London to see Dr. Albert Schweitzer on one of his visits to England and to learn about conditions from him. He kindly gave me the information I wanted. But I soon realized that the expenses of the undertaking would by a long way exceed my means—you do not make as much money on writing books as is generally believed. The images of an existence nine thousand feet up, under the long hill of Bardamat, among Masai children, dissolved like to other mirages above the grass.

The letters from my old servants in Africa would come in, unpredictably making their appearance in my Danish existence, strange, moving documents, although not much to look at. I wondered what would have made my correspondents feel just at that moment the necessity of walking in fifteen or twenty miles to Nairobi in order to send off these messages to me. At times they were dirges or elegies, at other times factual reports or even *chroniques scandaleuses*.

Two or three such epistles might follow quickly upon one another, then there might be many months in which the old continent was dumb.

But once a year at least I would be certain to get news of all my people.

From the time when I left Africa until the outbreak of the Second World War, every year before Christmas I sent out a small amount of money to my old firm of solicitors, Messrs. W. C. Hunter and Company, of Nairobi. They would always be able to get Farah's address, for he had his home and family in the Somali village of the town, even when he himself was away trading horses from Abyssinia or following some great white hunter on his safaris, and Farah would look up and collect his old staff. Thus in the white-washed Nairobi office my household was gathered together once more, each member of it was handed my Christmas present and was told to deliver in return, for my information, a short report on how he was and on what had happened to him in the course of the year. The bulletin, probably very slowly drawn from him, was put down by the clerk of the office in sober English and was easy to read, but had no voice to it.

But my people, inspired by what to them might seem an actual, renewed meeting with me—for the African has a capacity for disregarding distances of space and time—on leaving the solicitor's quarters laid their way round by the post-office, looked up the Indian professional letter-writer in his stall there and had this learned man set down for them a second message to me. In such way the letter, first translated in the mind of the sender from his native Kikuyu tongue into the lingua franca of Swahili, had later passed through the dark Indian mind of the scribe, before it was finally set down, as I read it, in his unorthodox English. Yet in this shape it bore a truer likeness to its author than the official, conventional note, so that as I contemplated the slanting lines on the thin yellow paper, I for a moment was brought face to face with him.

Juma wrote: "Some fire came into my house and ended one excellent goat." He also acquainted me with the negotiations around his daughter Mahô's marriage, speaking with scorn of the purchase price offered by her Kikuyu suitor. The moving passage about my predilection for little Mahô and the trouble I had taken to teach her to read obviously called for a reply from me, which might prove useful in the bargaining.

Ali Hassan, who had been personal boy to my mother when she had come out to visit me on the farm, during the Italian-Abyssinian war had accompanied General Llewellyn to Addis Ababa, and wrote: "Things was not very good here. If the old Memsahib was been in this place, this people would not behaved such as they do." Ali had Swahili blood in him, and the swift, incalculable manner of the Swahili. At first I had found him somewhat incongruous in my house. But he was steadier than he looked, a good worker, observant and with an unexpected mildness of mind.

Kamante wrote: "I got newly female infant from my wife, who is somewhat good sort."

Farah did not lay his way by the post-office. He will have dictated his letters in English himself. They were much like him, gravely and gracefully standing on his own dignity and mine, avoiding any manifestation of pity for any of us. He wrote about a parrot which he had purchased from an Indian friend as a present for me, and which could speak. When, he wrote, he had taught it a few more phrases and names of old mutual friends and acquaintances, if I was not coming back to Africa he would try to get it sent to Denmark. As in the end it proved to be impossible to realize this scheme, Farah gave the parrot to his mother-in-law, who all the time had much admired it, and sent me a few feathers plucked off it to show me what colour it had been. His personal feelings towards me, and the remembrance of our long acquaintance, came out in these letters, suddenly, and as in a new key, in the prayers to God for me preceding his signature.

Through these years I also kept up a correspondence with Abdullahi, my Somali servant, who by now was back in his own country. I have mentioned Abdullahi only very briefly before. Still he had for some years been a picturesque figure on the farm, with his own colours to him. I feel that he ought by now to be brought into the picture.

Abdullahi was Farah's small brother. He will have been ten years old by the time when Farah decided that the house needed a page more consistent with its dignity than the Kikuyu totos who till now had held the office, and had him sent down from Somaliland. Farah at first had asked for another boy, his sister's son, but the grandmother of the child, Farah's mother, had refused to part with him, for he was, she sent us word, of too high value to the tribe on account of his talent for tracking down camels which had strayed away at night. His mother's decisions to Farah were always unappealable, so it was Abdullahi Ahamed who one day appeared on my doorstep, and who for some years became one with the house.

In order to show his impartiality, Farah treated his little brother with sternness; a couple of times in the

Abdullahi

beginning of our acquaintance I felt called upon to take the side of the child. But in this, as in much of Farah's attitude and activity as major-domo, there was a good deal of pose, for the bond of blood to all Somali is supreme and sacred, and when at the time of the Spanish flu Abdullahi lay ill, Farah worried over him like a cat with her kitten. The two together made me think of Joseph and Benjamin, the Viceregent of Egypt laying his hand on the shoulder of the little Bedouin and speaking: "God be gracious to thee, my son."

Abdullahi had a round, chubby face, an unusual thing in a Somali, and a self-effacing manner, behind which one guessed weighty latent reserves. He was a loyal servant to the house, particularly pleasant to me because he was personally so clean and neat, and because I found in him a rare talent for gratitude. His individuality first manifested itself in an unexpected skill as a chess player. He stood by, quiet as a mouse, while Denys and Berkeley, who both considered themselves superior players, sat by the board. When questioned he told them that he knew the game of chess, and when, experimentally, they took him on as an opponent, he played in unbroken silence and almost invariably won his game.

Later on I found him to be a talented arithmetician as well. Denys had left an Oxford book of mathematics in the house. If I read out to Abdullahi one of its problems: "Divide up a number in four parts, so that the one part plus 4, the second part divided by 4, the third multiplied by 4, and the fourth part minus 4 will produce the same result," he sank into a kind of dumb ecstasy, and the next day would bring me the solution without being able to explain how he had arrived at it.

When Abdullahi had been at Ngong for a year he confided to me his passionate ambition to go to school. I felt it to be in a way legitimate, but since there was no Mohammedan school in the Highlands, I should have to send him to the Islamic school in Mombasa, and at the time I could ill afford to do so. When I told him: "I have not got the money, Abdullahi," he took in the fact resignedly, but from time to time, on an evening when Farah was not in the house, he came up to ask me: "Have you got more money now, Memsahib?"

Abdullahi's period of service in the house was marked by one dramatic event. I had been ordered by the doctor to take six drops of arsenic in a glass of water with my meals. When one day at lunch I had forgotten to do so

and sat reading in the library, I asked Abdullahi to pre-
pare and bring the dose, took the glass from him without
looking up from my book, and at the moment when I
drank down its contents realized that it must have been
filled with pure arsenic. I asked Abdullahi about it, and
he told me, stiffening, that it was so. I did not feel ill at
the time, only strangely stunned, as if I had received a
blow. "Then I think that I shall die, Abdullahi," I said,
"and you must send Farah in to me." Later on, Farah
told me that his little brother had come rushing into
his house, had cried out: "I have killed Memsahib! Go
in to her, you! And goodbye to you all, for I am going
away and am never coming back," and with these words
had vanished. By the time when Farah came, I myself
had really begun to believe that I was going to die. I
made him carry me on to my bed, and my agony there
grew worse and lasted for more than twelve hours. I
had no knowledge of arsenic poisoning and no instruc-
tions in my books of how to treat it. But after a while I
bethought myself of Alexandre Dumas' novel *La Reine
Margot*, which I had got in the house. This book tells
of how treacherous enemies of King Charles IX smear
the pages of a book on stag-hunting with arsenic, so that

the King, continuously wetting his finger to turn them, is slowly poisoned, and it also mentions the remedy by which the physician-in-ordinary tries to save the King's life. I had Farah find *Queen Margot* on my bookshelf, managed to look up the cure of milk and white-of-egg used, and started upon it, Farah lifting up my head so that I might swallow the medicine. In the midst of the treatment I remembered having been told that great quantities of arsenic will turn the patient a livid blue. In case it was really so, I reasoned, it was hardly worth struggling for life, so I sent for Kamante and had him stand by the bed, from time to time holding up my mirror to me. About midnight I began to think that I might after all remain alive, and about dawn to wonder about how we were to get Abdullahi back. Only after three days did the Masai scouts set on his track bring him in, the picture of a run-down, stunned scapegoat pardoned back from the desert.

When Abdullahi had been with me for three or four years, an event, small in itself, changed his fate.

In those days it was difficult to get a book to read in Nairobi. My bookseller would tell me that he had just got a beautiful consignment of books out from home, and then place before me a pile of such poor printed matter as seemed a shame to have good, seaworthy ships bring out. All the same it has twice there happened to me to pick up a book by an entirely unknown author, and the day after to write home telling my people to note down the author's name. The first of the two was Aldous Huxley's *Crome Yellow*, the second Ernest Hemingway's *The Sun Also Rises*. Now Huxley's *Little Mexican* was published. Among the tales of this book is the story "Young Archimedes," telling of a little boy with a genius for mathematics, by a vain and silly adoptive mother prevented from studying it and driven into such despair that in the end he throws himself from a balcony and dies. The night after I had read it I woke up almost as terrified as when I had left the baby bushbuck Lulu to her fate in the hands of Kikuyu totos. Within the following week I managed to scrape money together, and had Abdullahi sent off to the high school of Mombasa. He was very happy there, and his teachers wrote me that he was progressing steadily and beautifully.

Abdullahi travelled up from Mombasa a couple of times to visit us on the farm. He wore the clothes in which he had left us, and which by now had become somewhat scanty in length and short at the sleeves; he was evidently saving up his modest pocket-money for more books. These holiday visits after a year were rendered difficult by the fact that Farah had married, so that it had become illegal for Abdullahi to stay beneath his roof. In Somaliland, as in Jewry, when a man dies his younger brother marries his widow in order to raise up his seed, and I gathered that the close connection between a youthful brother and sister-in-law is considered dangerous as a possible incentive to fratricide. In a nation of such strict loyalty in family affairs the rule betrays a strange belief in the fatality of passion. I was sorry about the taboo, for I felt that Abdulluhi and Fathima, of the same age and both clear-eyed and easy-going, would have got on very well together *en tout bien tout honneur.*

When I left the country, Abdullahi did not care to stay there any longer either, but went back to Somaliland. From there he wrote to me, and I wrote back. He had not got Kamante's gift of letter-writing; his epistles to Denmark, beyond the fact that he was alive, gave little but a firm determination to hold on to me.

In the summer of 1936 I told him: "I am now writing a book about the farm. You are in it, and Farah, and Pooran Singh, and Bwana Finch-Hatton, and the dogs and Rouge. If I have good luck with this book, maybe I shall come back to Africa. So now you must pray to God for me." Abdullahi wrote back: "You need not tell me to pray to God for you, for that I do every day. But since in your letter you tell me that you are now writing a book about the farm, and that I am in it, and Farah and Pooran Singh, and Bwana Finch-Hatton, and the dogs, and Rouge, and that if you have good luck with this book maybe you will come back to Africa, I have set three very holy men on to pray for you every day. Then when these prayers are helpful to you, will you give me a typewriter?" What the three holy men were to get out of the arrangement I knew not, but felt that this must remain a matter between them and Abdullahi. My book *Out of Africa* was published in 1937 and had sufficient good luck, I decided, to bring me under an obligation towards Abdullahi, so I ordered a model typewriter for him in London, with his name on it. When the firm informed me that they could not guarantee its delivery, since from the last place to which they could forward it by post it must still travel for nine days on camel-back, I wrote to Abdullahi that he would have to arrange about the camel himself. He must have done so, for three months later I had a very neatly typed letter from him.

In the spring of 1939 I received a travelling grant, and began making up plans for travelling, in the month of Ramadan, with the pilgrims to Mecca, together with Farah and Farah's mother. On the farm Farah and I had many times discussed how, when we grew rich, we would go on such a pilgrimage, and had pictured to ourselves how we were to purchase excellent Arab horses, to obtain an escort from Ibn Saud and to journey happily through fair Arabia. Now I got as far as establishing contact with the Arabian Embassy in London.

Then with the Second World War, and with the German occupation of Denmark in April, 1940, I was quite suddenly cut off from both Arabia and Africa, as from humanity altogether.

The next two or three years stand out by nothing but

their nothingness; they look, today, like the Coalsack in the firmament of time. The King in his proclamation had enjoined us to maintain an attitude of calm and dignity, a prize was set on lying dead, a penalty on being alive.

All the same, impressions and reminiscences would drift into the Coalsack. A cultural gospel forced upon one, the status and name of protectorate imposed upon one's country. A new recognition of the importance of ancient traditions, of a three-thousand-year-old truth: "Honour thy father and thy mother: that thy days may be long upon the land which the Lord thy God giveth thee." In the Coalsack I unexpectedly encountered an old acquaintance, the *kipanda,* in the shape of that identification-card which each inhabitant of the country had to carry wherever he or she went. Through it I came to know for certain—what till then I had only guessed—that to be thus turned perfectly flat, two-dimensional, is extremely boring and may well make you feel the risk of being bored to death.

For my own part, in order to save my reason, I had recourse to the remedy which, for that same purpose, I had used in Africa in times of drought: I wrote a novel.

I advised my friends to do the same, for it took one's mind off German soldiers drilling in gas-masks round one's house and setting up their barracks on one's land. When I started on the first page of the book, I had no idea whatever what was going to happen in it, it ran on upon its own and—as was probably inevitable under the circumstances—developed into a tale of darkness. But when in the summer of 1943 the German persecution of Danish Jews set in, and most homes along the coast of the Sound were housing Jewish fugitives of Copenhagen waiting to be got across to Sweden, I slackened in my work; it began to look crude and vulgar to me to compete with the surrounding world in creating horrors. Also, as in the following months the Danish resistance movement fetched headway, we all began to rise from our sham graves, drawing the air more freely and ceasing to gasp for breath. My lifesaving book on its own put on a happy ending and—since I looked upon it as a highly illegitimate child—it was published under the pseudonym of Pierre Andrézel.

I gave much thought, all during those dark years, to my African servants. I held on to them to have them

prove to me that they were still there. They would be
moving about and talking; I tried to follow their movements and to hear what they were talking about. On
their new Dagoretti farms, would they be discussing
old days and asking one another, gravely, in the manner of the priest in church: "Do you believe in the
communion of the past? Do you believe in life gone
by?"

It was then that my old companions began to put in
an appearance in my dreams at night, and by such behaviour managed to deeply upset and trouble me. For
till then no living people had ever found their way into
those dreams. They came in disguise, it is true, and as
in a mirror darkly, so that I would at times meet Kamante in the shape of a dwarf-elephant or a bat, Farah
as a watchful leopard snarling lowly round the house,
and Sirunga as a small jackal, yapping—such as the
Natives tell you that jackals will do in times of disaster
—with one forepaw behind his ear. But the disguise
did not deceive me, I recognized each of them each
time, and in the mornings I knew that we had been together, for a short meeting on a forest path or for a
journey. So I could no longer feel sure that they did

still actually exist, or indeed that they had ever actually existed, outside of my dreams.

People work much in order to secure the future; I gave my mind much work and trouble, trying to secure the past.

And then, in the end, the Liberation came.

As now the dark, slimy waters began to decrease, Noah from his Ararat gazed round towards the four corners of the earth for a sprig of green.

The first live leaf was brought me all across the Atlantic. I had finished my *Winter's Tales* in 1942, when it had been out of the question to get the manuscript off to England or America from Denmark. By rare good luck, and with the aid of mighty friends, I managed to get it with me to Stockholm and to make the British Embassy there forward it by their daily plane. I wrote to my publishers in London and New York: "I can sign no contract and I can read no proofs. I leave the fate of my book in your hands." For three years I lived in the ignorance of that irresponsible person who shot an arrow into the air and left it to fall to earth he knew not where. Now, in the fair month of May, 1945, by one of the very first overseas mails, I received my book in the Armed Services Edition and shortly after, through the Red Cross, a number of moving and cheering letters from American officers and soldiers who had happened to read *Winter's Tales* just before or after some attack in Italy or the Philippines. I gave one of my two copies to the King, who was pleased to know that from his dumb country one voice at least had been heard in far places.

I sent a dove off south: I wrote to Messrs. Hunter and Company for information about my servants. They wrote back to inform me that Farah had died, and that without him they were unable to get on to any of the others.

The news of Farah's death to me was hard to take into my mind and very hard to keep there. How could it be that he had gone away? He had always been the first to answer a call. Then after a while I recognized the situation: more than once before now I had sent him ahead to some unknown place, to pitch camp for me there.

As to the others of my staff, now that I should no longer have Farah to look them up, it would, I reflected, be for them to find me. At the same time I could not be sure whether they would indeed set to do so or not. For they might not have grasped the fact that my long silence had been involuntary, but might quite well have taken it as a sign of my displeasure with them. "I shall have to sit still and wait for them," I thought, "as I waited at sunset for the bushbuck to step out into the glades of my grounds."

A few months later I had a letter from Government House in Nairobi, with the very coat of arms of Great Britain on it. Sir Philip Mitchell, the then Governor, told me that he was writing upon the repeated request of his boy Ali Hassan. Ali, he said, was the best servant he had ever had, but from the beginning he had made it clear to his master that he looked upon himself as still being in my service, and that if ever I came back to Africa he would feel free to leave Government House without notice.

Here Ali at least had come forth, then, in great state, accompanied by the Lion and the Unicorn. He would order the others back as well, and we would all be gathered together once more. I started on a correspondence with Ali. From the style of his letters I gathered that for these years he had—in contrast to earlier days —been living in a household with no financial worries. But he was faithful to the past, naming the horses and the dogs and bringing back things that I myself had forgotten. "Do you remember," he wrote, "how the people give you name and call you: She who first of all see the New Moon?" In his repeated "things have changed" there was a gentle melancholy, which I recognized from the recollections of other Africans, who will dwell with preference on sad things. There was in his letter the sound of a lonely horn in the woods, a long way off.

He generously forgave me my own *faux pas*. "Do you remember, Memsahib," he wrote, "the time when you dismissed us all because of this bitch?" I remembered it very well. I had brought out a Scotch deerhound bitch for my dog Pania, travelling, for her sake, in the midst of winter from Antwerp on a cargo boat. The first time she was in heat I had had to go into Nairobi, so had instructed all my servants, whatever they did, not to let her out of her hut. I came back tired and went to bed, and I there received a note from my manager regretting the fact that Heather had been let out, and that now most likely his Airedale terrier King would be the sire of her puppies. I at once flew into such anger that I walked straight from my bed on to the pergola, in which my entire household, sitting peacefully together, were having a sunset chat. But when I opened my mouth to tell them what I thought of them, I had no voice, I had to go back into the house to find it, and even to repeat the manœuvre. As soon as I could speak, I dismissed all my people at one time, for I felt that I could not bear to see any of their faces again. None of them went, or—I believe—for a moment thought of going, and no catastrophe followed. Whatever had happened in my absence, Heather's puppies turned out pure-bred, and very lovely.

Juma, Ali wrote, was now a very old man, with grandchildren and great-grandchildren. He lived upon the plot in the Masai Reserve that I had obtained for him. His son Tumbo was a lorry-driver in Nairobi.

Saufe, Farah's son, was doing well as a horse-trader. He was soon going to marry, and as he was only seventeen years old by then, the fact was a sign of his prosperity.

The news of Kamante, Ali wrote, was good, then bad, then a little better, then again somewhat sad. He had been clever all these years, "same as he been in the house," and on his land near Dagoretti he had a fine herd of cattle, sheep and goats. But he had gone blind. This, according to a clever doctor of Nairobi, might be bettered by an operation. But an operation would cost much money.

I found, as I laid down Ali's letter, that I was not surprised to learn that Kamante had gone blind. His watchful eyes, so keenly observant that he had at times made me think of that "loyal servant" of Grimm's fairy-tale who had to wear a cloth round his eyes in order not to destroy what he gazed at, at the same time in an eerie way had in them the introspectiveness which you will find in the eyes of a blind man. I remembered, from our very first meeting, when I had knocked against the dying child on the plain, those glassy, patient eyes turned towards me, and I felt that I must have them light up once more, even although I myself was never again to meet their unbiased, stock-taking glance.

I have had news from my old servants later on, through other people, and at last from themselves.

Sir Philip Mitchell in the beginning of the fifties looked me up in Denmark. "I dare not come home from Europe to Ali," he said, "without having seen you." While we dined together we had a sad little talk about the changes in the world. I realized to what extent my own book about Africa had become history, a document of the past. It was, I thought, as I listened to Sir Philip describing present-day conditions in Kenya, as much out of date as a papyrus from a pyramid.

My old friend Negley Farson in his book of 1950, *Last Chance in Africa*, speaks of Ali as Sir Philip's major-domo and reports how, at his and Sir Philip's fishing camp on the Thika, Ali repeats his statement that he is Memsahib Blixen's boy. "I rose," Mr. Farson tells, "high in Ali's esteem when I told him that I had lunched in

Denmark with his Memsahib. After that I could do no wrong."

The Danish author John Buchholzer in 1955 travelled in Somaliland to collect Somali folklore and poetry, and published a book, *Africa's Horn,* on his journey. One chapter of the book turns upon the new national and religious movement against the Europeans and relates how, in the market-place of the small town of Hargeisa, the author is being stoned by an angry crowd and is saved from their hands through the intervention of a passing young Somali official. The young man next day looks him up in his quarters and asks him if really, as has been said, he is a Dane. He presents himself as Abdullahi Ahamed, for many years in the past the servant of a Danish lady known to all tribes of Somali. Abdullahi here, in the book, goes through the long list of my benefactions towards him, including the typewriter.

It was pleasant to come across this passage of the book. It was more pleasant still to receive a letter from Abdullahi himself, inspired by his meeting with Mr. Buchholzer. For ten years, Abdullahi states, he has been deeply grieving not to hear from me; it now gives him much satisfaction that I have sent out such a nice gentleman to re-establish contact between us. He has actually married Farah's young widow and has a small son by her. The whole family, however, he informs me, is at the moment sunk in deep sadness over the death of Fathima's mother, the child's grandmother—so that old women appear to play as great a part in the life of the tribes as in my day. In his letter to me, too, Abdullahi remembers the typewriter. It gave him, he says, a decisive advantage over competitors in the career, and he owes to it that he has now for three years been holding the office of judge in Hargeisa.

"I am," he concludes his letter, "carrying my official duties successfully, with dignity and popularity."

There lives in Copenhagen a talented young journalist, Mr. Helge Christensen, who from boyhood has been keen on ornithology and many years ago got my mother's permission to study bird life in the woods of Rungstedlund. Mr. Christensen in an international competition won a flying trip to Nairobi and came to Rungstedlund to ask me whether I wanted him to take out greetings to friends of mine in Kenya. I asked him, if possible, to look up Juma and Kamante. But Ali Hassan being away at the time, I felt that it might be a difficult task to pick out by their names only two Kikuyu among two millions. Mr. Christensen, though, held on to his promise and was successful.

Juma he tracked down by going out to the residential district of Karen, named after me, and making enquiries at its central club-house, formerly my own house. He was here told that an old man by the name of Juma from time to time would come up and ask permission to walk in the grounds, "to think, there, of the time that had once been," for an afternoon would walk on the paths beneath the tall trees and then again would disappear. A kitchen toto from the club believed that he knew from where the old man came, and was taken into the car to point out the rough grass-track winding into the Masai Reserve—a long way, the traveller thought, for an old man to walk in order to meditate on the past. Juma's manyatta here, below the blue hills of Ngong, surely is one of the loveliest spots in the world. It had, Mr. Christensen told me, grown into a big place and was swarming with young people and children, who thronged round the car. Juma himself was called forth from his hut, a patriarch, full of days, somewhat long in the teeth, a little vague about the present but brightening up as he got on to days gone by, and in the end explaining to his wives and his off-spring that his Memsahib had sent out this good Bwana with gifts, thanksgivings for his excellent service in her house. Two eagles, Mr. Christensen told me, circling high above the heads of host and visitor, were pointed out as old friends of the Memsahib's, eager to have news of her. Juma once had heard them cry "God bless her." The scream of an eagle, as I myself heard it on a day when I was flying with Denys Finch-Hatton, is like anything but a blessing.

Kamante was found further away from Nairobi, in the midst of the maze of shambas with hemp, corn and sweet potatoes, and of grass-land. I was told that he received his visitor as if he had been expecting him this very afternoon, which may well have been the case, for Kamante was resourceful. Kamante had never shown any faith whatever in my intelligence, yet he now en-larged upon my wisdom and competence, pointing out to my countryman the wide area of land which, against all resistance and intrigue, I had forced the Govern-

ment of Kenya to yield up to him. Like Abdullahi and
Juma he took it that his guest had been sent out as a
personal ambassador of mine to get his news and enquire into his wants. He was anxious to send back by
him such news and information as I should be inter-
ested in, weighing his words and from time to time
making a pause to collect his thoughts. The operation
on his eyes had been successful, inasmuch as he could
now see his cows. He could not count them, he said,
which was a sad thing, but when in the evening they
had been brought back into their boma he could make
them out dimly, like a multitude of sweet potatoes
within a pot of furiously boiling water, thronging and
rolling about and jumping upon one another, which
was pleasant.

Mr. Christensen has published a small book, *Juma
and Kamante*, on his visit to my two old servants. It
contains two woodcut portraits of the title-characters;
the one of Juma is very good.

Quite recently, and quite by chance, I have in another Danish paper come upon a later interview with
Kamante, whom the journalist has succeeded in tracing
and running to earth. Kamante is well, and would like

to come to Denmark to take service with me once more, at the same time he fears that he is too old, and that it might be better to send me one of his sons. Somewhat uneasy at giving the information—as I am uneasy at passing it on here—Kamante tells the Danish journalist that he has been a year in prison for taking the Mau-Mau oath. I did not know of the circumstance; it has given me matter for thought. Has the deep, uncon-querable sceptic here at last met with something in which it was possible to him to have faith? Has the eternal hermit, the "rogue" head of game, by his own choice totally isolated from the herd, here at last through a dark inhuman formula experienced some kind of human fellowship? In order to make up for the awkwardness of the situation, Kamante brings out from his pocket a letter from me to him and shows it to my countryman. "Look," he says, "Msabu writes to me: 'My good and faithful servant Kamante.'" As again he folds up the letter and sticks it into his pocket, he adds: "And so I am."

I have had news of another former resident of the farm, the blind Dane, Old Knudsen, who for some time lived in a small house on it, all salted and embittered through the experiences of a tragic life, but with great flaming inner visions to make up for his loss of sight, a grey and bent indomitable optimist.

Last March I had a letter from an American lady of the University of Maryland. A fortnight before, she had been dining with a Danish economist just back from a recent mission to East Africa; they had been talking about me and my book *Out of Africa,* and he had told her that at the Danish Consulate to Tanganyika he had been given information which he wanted to bring to my attention. When a few days later he had died in his hotel in Washington, Mrs. Stevenson passed on this information to me. "What he had learned from the Danish Consul," she wrote, "and what I feel that he would want you to know, was that Old Knudsen's scheme for extracting phosphate from the bottom of Lake Naivasha was *not* wild. Some discovery has been made which verifies his theory. I did not get the details, but I feel that you should know."

Thus, with deep satisfaction, I now see before me Old Knudsen righted, for a while laying down his harp in order to grip old fishermen's and mariners' tools, laughing out in triumph over Old Knudsen's enemies.

I hear, these days, with intervals of one month, or half a year, from my old servants in Africa.

So there they are, out from their coverts in the woods, in the rays of sunset, treading cautiously still, but looking round them more confidently than when they first came into sight, lifting and turning their heads. It is content to watch you so, friends and comrades, I wish you may wander and gaze there, so high up in the air, in the strange freedom of your hearts, for a long time still. You have kept me company through many years; I shall not again frivolously doubt your actuality, I shall, from now, leave to you the rich world of reality. And you may hand me over to those dreams of mine which will take charge of me.

Juma has died. But I have recent news of Ali and Kamante.

Ali writes good English now. He has seen my photograph in the paper. "Really and truthfully it makes my heart very much pleased to see your photo. Really and truthfully it fills all my heart with joy when I hear your name spoken. Or when I speak your name."

As I admire his handwriting and grammar, I sometimes seem to see Berkeley's little wry smile as in his mind he followed a line of wild duck on the glass-clear sky. And I wonder whether one more of them, fascinated by the decoys below, will here be slowing its flight to drop, in the end, like an arrow-head let off backwards by some heavenly archer, into the water of the pond, in order to become respectable.

But Kamante, all through a triple layer of idiom, in a many-times-folded note, manages to preserve his originality. His last letter, of a month ago, ends up:

"I certainly convinced when I pray for you to almighty God that this prayer he will be stow without fault. So I pray that God will be kind to you now and then."

About the Author

ISAK DINESEN is the *nom de plume* of Baroness Karen Blixen of Rungstedlund. Born of an old Danish family, she has carried forward its tradition of making contributions to Danish literature while establishing a distinguished niche for herself in English as well as Danish letters. Her father gained distinction as a writer after he had served as an army officer and had come to America, where he lived for several years as a trapper with the Pawnee Indians in Minnesota. Two of his books were published in Denmark under the pseudonym of Boganis, a title conferred upon him by the Pawnees. Her brother, Thomas Dinesen, a soldier in the First World War and also an author of repute, was awarded the Victoria Cross for extraordinary valor.

The author of *Anecdotes of Destiny* was married to a cousin, Baron Blixen, in 1914 and went with him to British East Africa, where they established and successfully operated a coffee plantation. In 1921 she was divorced from her husband, but she continued to manage the plantation for another ten years, until the collapse of the coffee market forced her to sell her property and go back to Denmark. Her book *Out of Africa* records many of her experiences in the Colony with a painter's feeling for its sweeping landscapes and a sure-handed wizardry in communicating the character of its people. It was selected by the Book-of-the-

Month Club and was received with acclaim by critics and readers alike.

Prior to the publication of *Out of Africa,* Isak Dinesen had established a firm place for herself in America with her first book, *Seven Gothic Tales.* That volume and *Winter's Tales,* her second collection of stories, were also Book-of-the-Month Club selections. Her third collection, *Last Tales,* was published in 1957.

In 1957 Isak Dinesen was elected to honorary membership in the American Academy and National Institute of Arts and Letters. Reserved for foreigners who have made unusual contributions to the arts, honorary memberships in the academy-institute are limited to fifty.